in the Sprubly Islands

Poog

Gax

Akiko

Mr. Beeba

Spuckler

in the Sprubly Islands

Written and illustrated by

MARK CRILLEY

DELACORTE PRESS

Published by Delacorte Press
an imprint of
Random House Children's Books
a division of Random House, Inc.
1540 Broadway
New York, New York 10036

Visit us on the Web! www.randomhouse.com/kids
Educators and librarians, for a variety of teaching tools,
visit us at www.randomhouse.com/teachers

Library of Congress Cataloging-in-Publication Data
Crilley, Mark.
    Akiko in the Sprubly Islands / written and illustrated by Mark Crilley.
       p.   cm.
    Summary: Ten-year-old Akiko and her newly made friends survive a skug-
bit storm, crash in the Moonguzzit Sea, and are captured by the army of
Queen Pwip as they continue their mission to rescue the son of the king of
the planet Smoo.
    ISBN 0-385-32726-9
    [I. Science fiction. 2. Life on other planets—Fiction. 3. Adventure and
adventurers—Fiction. 4. Japanese Americans—Fiction.] I. Title.
PZ7.C869275 Ak 2000
[Fic]—dc21   00-029518

The text of this book is set in 15-point Centaur.
Book design by Debora Smith
Manufactured in the United States of America
September 2000
10 9 8 7 6 5 4 3 2 1
BVG

For my wife, Miki.
"Zutto zutto"

ACKNOWLEDGMENTS

As always, many thanks are due to Robb Horan, Larry Salamone, and Joseph Michael Linsner of Sirius Entertainment, whose faith in Akiko and the gang has remained steadfast through many a hair-raising adventure. I must thank not one but two editors: Lawrence David, who, with his usual wisdom and grace, got this book off to the best possible start, and Fiona Simpson, who cheerfully supplied the guidance and encouragement I needed to make it across the finish line. I am very much indebted to Andrew Smith, who was among the very first to envision Akiko as a series of children's books, and whose support was instrumental in getting the project off the ground. Thanks also to Debora Smith for patiently listening to my requests to put "this drawing here, and that drawing . . . right there!" A big bouquet of thank-yous for the following friends of Akiko at Random House Children's Books: Judith Haut, Daisy Kline, Angela Adams, So Lin Wong, Kerry Moynagh, Barbara Perris, and Gabriel X. Ashkenazi. And finally, big kisses for my wife, Miki, followed by little kisses for my son, Matthew, who (when he's old enough to read) will, I hope, find this book to his liking.

Chapter 1

I opened my eyes. I'd been sleeping so soundly that for the first few seconds I had no idea where I was. Then it slowly came back to me: I was on the planet Smoo with my new friends Spuckler Boach, Gax, Mr. Beeba, and Poog. We were floating peacefully above the clouds on our little flying boat, resting up before the next leg of our journey.

I was a little embarrassed to notice that everyone else was already awake. Mr. Beeba was steering the boat, Poog was floating quietly by himself just behind the mast, and Spuckler was giving Gax a little tune-up. (After all that poor robot had been through lately, I'm sure he needed it.)

"Hey there, Akiko," said Spuckler, smiling as always. "How ya doin'? Feels good to get a little shut-eye, don't it?"

"Yeah," I said, yawning and stretching my arms. "How long was I asleep?"

"Not *particularly* long," Mr. Beeba said, turning his head to join the conversation. "You've nothing to be ashamed of, dear girl. I would encourage you to get all the rest you can."

"Yeah, 'Kiko," Spuckler agreed. "'Cause there ain't nothin' *else* to do on this boat."

"You have *entirely* misconstrued the meaning of my statement, Spuckler," Mr. Beeba said wearily.

"I'm *right*, though," Spuckler insisted.

"You most certainly are *not*," Mr. Beeba answered. He was never one to pass by a good argument with Spuckler. And who was I to stop him? Watching the two of them go at it was as good as any television show. Poog was interested too, apparently. He floated over and gave himself a good view of the debate.

"I'm sure there are any *number* of interesting activities

for an intelligent child like Akiko to do on a boat such as this," Mr. Beeba continued.

"Name two," Spuckler grunted, tightening a bolt on Gax's underside.

"Well," Mr. Beeba began, "she could practice memorizing the names of all the books I've written—"

"That don't count," Spuckler interrupted. "You said *interesting.*"

"She could follow *that* up," Mr. Beeba continued, ignoring Spuckler for the moment, "by memorizing passages from the books themselves."

"Well, that just proves my point," said Spuckler victoriously. "There ain't nothin' for 'Kiko to do on this boat but *sleep.*" Gax clicked and whirred quietly as Spuckler tightened another bolt underneath his helmet.

"Hmpf!" Mr. Beeba snorted, apparently losing interest in the argument. There was a long pause, during which neither of them said anything. I found myself staring at the clouds and secretly agreeing with Spuckler.

After a long while I saw some orange-winged creatures flying overhead. They were the same creatures I'd seen way back when we'd just begun our journey.

"Hey, look, Mr. Beeba," I said, pointing up at them as they passed over us. "There's some more of those reptile-bird things you were telling me about before."

"Yumbas, Akiko. *Yumbas*," he replied, sounding slightly disappointed that I hadn't remembered the name. "An odd species, actually. All Yumbas fly in precisely the same direction by instinct. Northeast, I believe. Or was it southwest? Well, in any case, it is said that the average Yumba literally circles the planet once every fourteen days."

"No kidding," I said, shielding my eyes from the sun as I watched the Yumbas fly off into the distance. "Where I come from, birds fly in pretty much any direction they want." I thought for a moment about my science teacher, Mrs. Jackson, back at Middleton Elementary. She had this big lesson plan one time about birds and how they fly south in the winter. She actually took us out into the school yard so that we could see real birds flying south. We didn't end up seeing anything, though, and all I remember is how cold it was and how I wanted to get back into the classroom as quickly as possible.

I leaned back on my elbows and looked up at the clouds again, wondering what direction the Yumbas were flying in. I wondered if they got tired of seeing the same scenery over and over again.

Then a really weird thing happened. A second flock of Yumbas passed overhead, and I thought for sure they were crossing over us in a slightly different direction. The time before, they had come from the left-hand side of the ship and had flown across to the right. This time it was just a little more from the front of the ship, heading toward the back. I sat there and waited to see if more Yumbas would pass overhead.

Sure enough, another group flew over us, and this time it was even more obvious that they were changing direction.

"Hey, Mr. Beeba," I said, "I think you might be wrong about those Yumbas."

"Me?" Mr. Beeba asked, as if I'd just proposed something altogether impossible. *"Wrong?"*

"It's nothing personal, Mr. Beeba," I explained cautiously. "I just think that maybe sometimes they fly in more than one direction."

"Really, Akiko," Mr. Beeba clucked disapprovingly. "It's one thing to postulate a theory contrary to my own, but quite another to do so without offering any proof whatsoever to back it up."

"Well, look up there and see what I'm talking about," I said, pointing at yet another group of Yumbas in the sky. Mr. Beeba coughed, cleared his throat, and watched as they passed over us, this time coming a little from the right and heading slightly to the left.

There was a long, awkward silence as Mr. Beeba followed the path of the Yumbas with his eyes.

"Inconceivable!" he said at last, scratching agitatedly at his head. "Yumbas *never* change direction."

"Now, wait a gol-darned second here," Spuckler said, jumping to his feet.

Mr. Beeba and I turned around to face him, a little surprised that he had any interest whatsoever in the conversation. Spuckler paced back and forth across the deck, looking up at the clouds and down at the Moonguzzit Sea beneath us, a very grim expression coming over his face. Gax watched him nervously, as if experience had taught him to be prepared for sudden drastic changes in Spuckler's mood.

"Those birds ain't changin' directions," he announced. "*We* are!"

"Us?" Mr. Beeba asked, his eyes widening. "You mean the *ship*? Don't be ridiculous!" There was a slightly uneasy sound in his voice, though, as if some terrible truth had just begun to dawn on him.

"We're goin' around in *circles* is what we're doin',"

Spuckler said, now starting to sound angry. "No *wonder* we been flyin' all this time and we still ain't past the Moonguzzit Sea!"

"F-flying in circles?" Mr. Beeba stuttered. "Nonsense! I've been steering this ship in an absolutely straight line!"

"You don't get it, do ya, Beebs?" Spuckler exclaimed, throwing his arms up in the air. "We are lost! *L-A-W-S-T,* lost!"

"We . . . ," Mr. Beeba began, trying rather desperately to defend himself, "we'd have *finished* this mission

by now if your Sky Pirate friends hadn't destroyed all my books!"

"Aw, you an' your stupid books!" Spuckler said. He was actually kind of shouting. "You ain't in your cozy little *library* anymore, Beebs. This is *reality* out here— take a good look!"

This argument seemed more serious than the little spats I'd seen so far, and I figured if I didn't interrupt they'd end up throwing punches or something. I cleared my throat and jumped in between the two of them.

"Look, we're never going to get anywhere if you two don't stop *arguing* all the time!"

Without even a pause, they stopped, turned, pointed at each other, and said (at exactly the same time), "*He* started it."

Honestly! You'd think they were first-graders or something.

"I don't care *who* started it," I said, putting on my best bossy voice and wagging a finger in front of both of them. "I'm in charge of this mission and I *order* you to stop fighting."

And it worked, too. They both got quiet and just

stared at the deck for a minute. A soft breeze blew over us and flapped through the sails as I allowed the silence to continue a little bit longer. The sun was getting lower in the sky, and we were all covered in a warm yellow glow.

"All right," I said finally. "We're going to sit right down here and have a little meeting."

"A meetin'?" Spuckler asked, with obvious disapproval.

"Yes. We're going to talk about how we got into this mess. Then we're going to find a way out of it." This was a little trick I'd learned from my history teacher, Mr. Moylan, back at Middleton Elementary. He said you always need to have a little meeting like this whenever you're in a tough situation and you can't figure out what to do next. Under the circumstances I think he'd have agreed this was a pretty good time to follow his advice.

Chapter 2

"Okay," I said, trying to use a very businesslike voice, "the first thing we have to do is decide whether or not we're really lost."

"We're *lost*, all right," Spuckler snapped.

"Quiet, Spuckler," I snapped back at him. "If you want to say something at this meeting you have to raise your hand."

Spuckler rolled his eyes and Mr. Beeba smiled triumphantly.

"Now, Mr. Beeba," I continued, trying to think of a gentle way to approach the subject. "Are you willing to admit that we *might* be lost?"

Mr. Beeba pulled a handkerchief out from beneath his belt and began cleaning his spectacles. He took his time answering, as if he enjoyed making us all wait for him.

"We may possibly be a *tad* off course, yes," he said quietly, focusing most of his attention on a smudge he was trying to remove from one of the lenses.

"A *tad?*" Spuckler snorted.

"*Please*, Spuckler," I said, glaring at him. "It doesn't do us any good to point fingers at one another. If we're lost, the most important thing is to get *un*-lost. Remember, Prince Froptoppit is out there locked up somewhere, and like it or not, we're his only hope of being rescued."

An air of helplessness fell over the whole group. Even Gax and Poog seemed perplexed.

"Now, any way you look at it, I've got to admit this mission of ours hasn't gone very smoothly so far. But at least we're all still together."

"Yes, quite," Mr. Beeba murmured, not sounding particularly pleased. There was a long pause, during

which Spuckler rubbed his chin and scratched at the back of his head.

"Now, Mr. Beeba," I asked, "is there any way you know of getting us back on course?"

"Tragically, no," Mr. Beeba replied, a dejected look coming over his face. "Though this vessel of ours is very charming, I'm afraid it is not equipped with the sort of navigational equipment we so desperately need at the moment."

There was another long pause as we all sat and tried to come up with a way out of our dilemma. Just when I was starting to think the whole meeting idea might turn out to be a big waste of time, Poog spoke up. It had been quite a while since he'd said anything, so I was a little startled to hear his warbly, high-pitched voice. It still impressed me that Mr. Beeba was actually able to understand Poog's bizarre alien language.

"Really?" Mr. Beeba asked in response to what Poog had just said. "Well, now, *that's* encouraging!"

Poog continued with another brief burst of syllables, then stopped and smiled, blinking his big black eyes once or twice.

"Poog has just informed me of someone who might be able to help us," Mr. Beeba announced, his voice now very hopeful. "Her name is Pwip. She's the Queen of the Sprubly Islands."

"The Sproobly Islands?" I asked.

"*Sprubly*, Akiko. Rhymes with 'bubbly.' It's a small chain of islands in the middle of the Moonguzzit Sea. Poog tells me that if we can find Queen Pwip, she might be able to show us how to get to the place where Prince Froptoppit is being held captive."

"You mean Alia Rellapor's castle?" I asked.

"Exactly," Mr. Beeba answered, a mysterious look coming over his face. "Not only that, but Queen Pwip is evidently something of a clairvoyant."

"What's a claire buoyant?" I asked, never having heard the word before.

"A *clairvoyant*, Akiko," he corrected, "is someone who has the ability to see or know things beyond the realm of normal perception. Queen Pwip, it seems, has just such an ability. She may even be able to foresee the future."

"Wow! She really *is* the sort of person we need," I said, sitting up straight. "Thank you, Poog, for telling us about her. I have a feeling this could make all the difference."

"Well, I don't know if I believe in fortune-tellers and all that kind of razzmatazz," Spuckler said, scratching his head again, "but if she can show us the way to Alia's castle, I reckon it's worth lookin' her up."

"That settles it, then," I said in an authoritative voice, bringing the meeting to a close. "Our mission for the time being is to look for the Sprubly Islands and find Queen Pwip!"

"Thank you, Akiko," Mr. Beeba whispered to me a moment later. "That was a *very* productive meeting."

Chapter 3

We all spent the rest of the afternoon looking down at the Moonguzzit Sea, hoping to catch a glimpse of the Sprubly Islands. Mr. Beeba even brought the ship down to a lower altitude so we'd get a clearer view. There was nothing to see, though, but clear blue water stretching off in all directions.

The air began to cool as the sun went down, and Spuckler prepared a light dinner from the food remaining in the ship's storage compartment. I ate a big piece of bread and four or five plump little pickles, and washed it all down with a bottle of turquoise liquid that tasted something like watermelon juice. Spuckler kept eating long after Mr. Beeba and I had finished. He only stopped when Mr. Beeba insisted that we had to ration the food for the days ahead.

After dinner we all sat back and enjoyed the sunset. It was one of the most beautiful sights I'd ever seen. The sky turned bright red and orange and the clouds went from white to blue to purple. The view we had was like something you'd see from up in an airplane, except instead of peeking through a tiny little window, I was able to look around in every direction and feel the breeze blowing across my face.

After sundown it got even better. One by one the stars began to appear, and before long the whole sky was covered with them. You could even see two or three planets nearby, each different shades of green and yellow. I'd never seen even *half* as many stars back in Middleton, even on the clearest night of the year. I thought briefly of my parents and wondered what they were doing. I wished I could see them or talk to them somehow, just to be sure they were okay.

Mr. Beeba started to give me a little astronomy lesson, but I was already much too sleepy to pay attention.

". . . and that one over there to the left," I heard him say as my eyes grew heavier and heavier, "is more than 375,000 light-years away. Mind you, I wouldn't blame you for thinking it a great deal closer. . . ."

"Let her sleep, Beeba," Spuckler whispered. "Poor girl's exhausted."

Spuckler threw a blanket over me and tucked it in all around my body. I opened my eyes and caught one last dazzling view of the stars before drifting off to sleep.

The next morning I awoke to find the sky dark gray, with big black clouds rolling in overhead. A strong wind whistled across the deck and my skin got goose-pimply all along my forearms. I pulled my blanket up around my shoulders, trying to stay warm.

"Mornin', 'Kiko," Spuckler said. "Weather's kinda turnin' against us today. Don't worry, though. A little rain never hurt no one."

I looked around and saw Mr. Beeba staring gloomily into the sky. Poog and Gax seemed relatively unaffected by the change in the weather, as if it didn't really matter to them one way or the other.

As the sky
got darker and darker,
Poog made an announcement.

"Heavens!" Mr. Beeba said as he
began to translate. "Poog says we're heading
into a skugbit storm!"

I had no idea what a skugbit storm was, but I could
tell by looking at Mr. Beeba's face that it was something
pretty bad.

"Now, hang on, everybody," Spuckler said. "Let's not
get worked up into a panic over this. Poog might be
wrong."

"Poog's never wrong!" Mr. Beeba warned.

"We'll see about that," said Spuckler, turning to his
trusty robot. "Gax, switch on your weather sensors and
see what's goin' on out there."

"WEATHER SENSORS?" Gax asked hesitantly. There
was an embarrassing pause, as if he had no idea what
Spuckler was talking about.

"OH, WEATHER SENSORS!" he added a second later, his head popping up a few inches in recognition. "JUST A MOMENT, SIR. I KNOW THEY'RE DOWN HERE SOME-WHERE. . . ." And with that he began searching through the various compartments and pieces of junk that were hidden inside his body.

Just then something dropped down and hit Gax right on the top of his helmet.

TWANG!

Spuckler reached out and caught it as it ricocheted into the air.

"Hang on, Gax," he said, "I think we got your forecast right here."

"What's that?" I asked, leaning over to get a better look.

"It's a skugbit," he answered, dropping it into my hand. It was a round rock, about the size of a golf ball, but covered with little scratches and pockmarks. It was also warm, as if its quick fall through the air had heated it up.

"When there's a storm, *millions* of these little suckers start fallin' down outta the sky," Spuckler added. The sky grew darker and we heard high-pitched whistling sounds as more and more skugbits began to whiz by the ship on all sides, some of them missing by just a few feet.

"Sh-should we be worried, Spuckler?" Mr. Beeba asked, looking nervously at the sky.

Suddenly there was a huge crash just a few feet away from me as an enormous skugbit smashed right down into the middle of the deck. Pieces of the deck shot up in all directions and the whole ship shuddered from the impact. The skugbit was about the size of a beach ball, or even bigger! We all circled around the monstrous thing and stared at it in horror.

"Yeah," Spuckler said, leaning over to inspect the damage, "if you're thinkin' about bein' worried, I'd say now's as good a time as any."

Chapter 4

Within a few minutes we were in the thick of the storm. Skugbits of all sizes were raining down on the ship, tearing great big holes in the sails. With each skugbit that landed on the deck, the ship dropped a bit lower in the sky, moving ever closer to the surface of the Moonguzzit Sea. Spuckler took charge of the situation.

"Throw 'em overboard, everybody!" he shouted, pointing at the dozens of skugbits that had accumulated on the deck. "They're weighin' down the ship!"

So we started throwing the skugbits overboard as fast as we could. They were incredibly heavy, though, and for every one or two we succeeded in getting off the deck, seven or eight came crashing down in their places. Even Spuckler, who had the muscles to work a lot faster than the rest of us, just couldn't keep up.

The ship dropped lower and lower under the weight of the skugbits. We sank slowly at first, then faster and faster until we reached a dizzying speed. Before long the waves of the Moonguzzit Sea were rushing up to meet us.

"Brace yourself, guys!" Spuckler hollered. "It's gonna be a rough landing!"

The ship hit the water so hard it almost broke in

half. Water poured over the sides and up through the holes that had been made by the skugbits. Soon we were all soaking wet, and the waves were lapping over the ship from all directions.

"Dear heavens, we're sinking!" I heard Mr. Beeba squeal as another wave came crashing down on top of us.

"Grab a piece and hang on!" Spuckler shouted back to him.

Before long the entire ship was submerged, leaving Spuckler and me clinging to a piece of the mast. Mr. Beeba ended up staying above water by clutching Gax (who turned out to be surprisingly seaworthy), and Poog hovered in the air just a foot or two above the spot where Spuckler and I were floating.

It had all happened so quickly that we didn't have a chance to think what we'd do next. Fortunately the skugbit storm began to blow over, so at least we didn't have to worry about more rocks crashing down on top of us.

However, we soon had something much more frightening to worry about.

Chapter 5

As we bobbed up and down in the freezing cold waters of the Moonguzzit Sea, we saw the surface begin to bubble and churn just a few yards away. Something was coming up from underneath us, something really, really big. The water started swelling and spraying high into the air. Then it was forced outward in all directions in a giant circular wave, finally falling away to reveal the head of a huge underwater creature! It towered about fifty feet above the sea, staring down at us with four black, glassy eyes. It had shiny skin like a dolphin, but its head was shaped like a giant slug, complete with thick, slimy antennae slowly twirling in the air.

"What . . . ," I gasped, ". . . what *is* that thing?"

"I ain't exactly sure," Spuckler replied. "But I sure hope it ain't hungry."

Hungry or not, the gigantic beast started coming after us, mouth open wide. We tried our best to swim away, but it was much too late for that. Plunging its mouth into the sea, the creature just sucked the five of us inside along with a large gulp of water. Before we knew it, we were sliding into the creature's throat and down into the darkness of its body, with nothing at all to slow our fall. It got darker and darker, and all I can remember is the sensation of falling and sliding, slipping through slimy passageways, being carried along by a wave of water and who-knows-what-else.

Finally I felt myself coming to a stop. I was lying on a slimy, spongy surface that felt like it was covered with a mixture of oil and algae. The air was heavy and moist, and there was a *very* unpleasant smell like rotting fish. It was so dark, I couldn't tell the difference between having my eyes open and keeping them shut.

A moment later there was a sudden flash of light just a few feet from my face. I jumped back and turned away

as my eyes adjusted to the brightness. With a big sigh of relief, I realized that the warm glow was coming from Gax.

"Hey, whaddya know, Gax?" Spuckler said, adjusting a knob on Gax's side. "This torch of yours still works!"

"YOU NEEDN'T SOUND SO *SURPRISED*, SIR," Gax replied, admiring the steady yellow flame that he had produced.

I looked around and saw Poog floating nearby, and Mr. Beeba flat on his back, his eyes still closed, his chest slowly rising and falling. It was a big relief to see that we were all still together.

"Spuckler!" I said as I crawled out of the shadows. "Are you okay?"

"Course I am!" he said with a grin. Knowing how much Spuckler liked adventure, he was probably *enjoying* all this stuff. "How 'bout you?"

"I'm all right, I guess. Where do you think we *are?*"

"I reckon we're right smack-dab between that snake's mouth and her belly," Spuckler answered calmly.

"No wonder it's so *gross* in here," I moaned, glancing around at the shiny pink walls. It looked like we were sitting inside a gigantic intestine or a throat or something equally slimy.

"Hey, Beebs!" Spuckler said, crawling over to Mr. Beeba. "C'mon, big guy, snap out of it!"

Mr. Beeba's eyes opened very slowly. He was still a little groggy.

"Spuckler?" he whispered, coughing once or twice. "Inconceivable! Even in *death* I can't escape you. . . ."

"Aw, you ain't dead, Beeba," Spuckler assured him. "You jus' got swallered up like the rest of us."

Mr. Beeba sat up and took a better look at his surroundings. Before long he seemed wide awake.

"Good heavens!" he said at last. "By the looks of these internal walls, we must be inside the belly of a Moonguzzit water snake. If I'm not mistaken, we've come to rest inside the *plipto-thotamus.*" Under the circumstances, I'd say Mr. Beeba was handling things pretty well. He was examining the surface of the walls as if he were a scientist sent down here to do research or something.

"Well, I don't know nothin' 'bout no plippy-whatzamus," said Spuckler, "but it sure is *gooey* in here. If you'd take us to the nearest exit, I'm sure we'd all be much obliged."

"Don't be ridiculous, Spuckler," Mr. Beeba scoffed. "We're probably *miles* beneath the water's surface by now." There was a pause as we all took in the frightening meaning of this statement. Gax whirred and rotated his head a bit, and Poog floated over to where I was sitting, as if to offer me some sort of protection.

"Besides," Mr. Beeba added, a pained expression coming over his face, "there's only one exit I know of, and it's . . . *most* disagreeable."

"We can't just *sit* here, Mr. Beeba," I said, a panicky tone coming into my voice. "We'll get . . . I don't know, *digested* or something."

"Girl's got a point, Beebs," said Spuckler, folding his arms in front of him. He seemed less frightened than simply uninterested in the confined surroundings.

"Well, I say we have a look around," Mr. Beeba replied. "There are bound to be some fascinating anatomical lessons to be learned down here."

Mr. Beeba started walking along the passageway, inspecting certain things very closely and saying stuff like "What have we here?" and "Indeed. Just as I suspected!" Spuckler gave me a knowing look, as if to say "Yeah, he's kind of a nutcase, ain't he?" Within seconds Mr. Beeba had made a very important discovery. Important to *him*, anyway.

"Look: the spleeductum gland!" he announced with a happy shout, pointing at a slimy little thing dangling above his head. It was round and pink and was slowly

expanding and contracting. I couldn't help thinking of those gross medical shows on TV where they stick a camera in somebody's body while they're having an operation. Mr. Beeba *caressed* the thing, though, as if it were a long-lost friend or something.

"Boys back at school thought I was perfectly *mad* when I suggested that a water snake had one of these."

"What's it do?" I asked, not sure I really wanted to know.

"Why, a great many things, Akiko," he answered, like a proud father. "I wrote my dissertation on the subject, as a matter of fact. First and foremost, it tells the mouth what to eat and what not to eat. . . ."

"You stupid gland!" Spuckler growled, pulling the thing down to his eye level. "You'll rue the day you crossed Spuckler Boach!"

Clearly it was time to move on. We all walked together from one passageway to the next, but it didn't seem to be getting us anywhere. For one thing, we had no idea if we were heading *out* of the creature's stomach or *into* it. Mr. Beeba knew all about glands and ventricles and stuff, but somehow he was still getting us completely lost.

"Since we took a left at the glorplaxia, we should have reached the troochea by now," he said, as much to himself as to anyone else. "You don't suppose this snake could have had a troochectomy, do you?"

"Well, gang," Spuckler said with a yawn, "I say we make camp here and take a load off our legs for a while."

"Good idea, Spuckler," I said. "I think we all need the rest."

Chapter 6

We all sat down on the spongy surface and tried to get as comfortable as possible. I couldn't really sleep, so I just sat there thinking about how badly the whole mission was going. I was starting to get homesick again too. Sure, it was nice to have made such interesting friends on the planet Smoo, but at that particular moment I'd have much rather been back on Earth. *Anywhere* back on Earth.

I stared into the darkness and thought about my parents. I wondered what they were doing. It was weird to think that they probably hadn't even noticed I was gone. As long as that look-alike Akiko robot was on Earth taking my place, they'd both just go about their daily routines as if nothing had changed. It bothered me to realize that I was missing them so much and they weren't missing me at all.

I started thinking about how badly I wanted just to see them for a minute or two, or talk to them by telephone or something. What if something really awful had happened to them while I was gone? It was certainly possible. There was no way of knowing one way or the other until I got back to Earth. And when would I *get* back to Earth, anyway? How many more days? Or would it turn out to be weeks? Or *months?* The more I thought about it, the more frustrated I became.

"Hey, 'Kiko," Spuckler said. "What's with the sad face? Things could be worse, trust me."

"You're right, Spuckler," I sighed. "I don't know what's wrong with me. I'm just thinking about things too much, I guess."

"That'll do it every time," Spuckler said. I think it's safe to say Spuckler makes it a practice *never* to think too much.

"Say, I know something that'll cheer you up," Spuckler continued, his face brightening. "Let's see if Poog will hum us a tune!"

"Poog can sing?" I asked. I was pretty intrigued, I have to admit. It had never occurred to me that Poog might be able to sing.

"Can he ever!" Spuckler answered. "Poog sings prettier'n anybody in the whole galaxy!

"C'mon, Beebs," he continued, turning to Mr. Beeba. "Make him sing that one I like, the one about the Toog Dogs."

"I can't *make* Poog do anything, Spuckler," Mr. Beeba replied indignantly. "He's not a *machine*."

Gax gave a little shudder after this last remark, and Mr. Beeba hastily added, "Er, no *offense*, Gax."

"NONE TAKEN, SIR," Gax replied graciously.

"Poog doesn't sing at the drop of a hat," Mr. Beeba explained, turning back to Spuckler. "He has to be in the right *mood*."

"Well, let's try'n *put* him in the right mood!" Spuckler suggested. You could tell he wasn't going to give up on the idea.

"It's a very subtle matter of *atmosphere,* Spuckler," Mr. Beeba said dismissively. "Quite beyond your understanding, I'm afraid."

"Gax," Spuckler said without a second's pause, "cool that torch of yours a little."

Gax immediately brought the fire on his torch down to a small, flickering glow, and suddenly it felt like we were in a dimly lit cave or something. There was a long pause. We all turned and looked at Poog, wondering if Spuckler's idea would do the trick.

Slowly we became aware of a quiet little hum coming from Poog, as if he were warming up. A moment later Poog began to sing.

I wish you could have heard it, because it's *really* hard to describe what it was like. It was a weird mix of clear,

high-pitched sounds, like flutes and crickets and other soft little noises all mixed together. One thing's for sure. It was just about the prettiest music I'd ever heard in my whole life.

I tried to stay awake, but Poog's singing was so peaceful and relaxing that I just couldn't resist closing my eyes. A minute or two later I fell into a deep, deep sleep.

Chapter 7

I don't know how long it was before I woke up. All I remember is that when I opened my eyes I found Spuckler and Mr. Beeba asleep, both of them snoring like crazy. Poog had stopped singing by then. He had his eyes closed and was just humming quietly to himself. As for Gax, he was wide awake. Robots always *are*, I guess. But he looked even more alert than usual, and I couldn't help thinking he was nervous about something.

"What's up, Gax?" I whispered, crawling over to him. "Are you okay?"

"I'm quite fine, ma'am," he answered. "it's my quake sensors; they seem to be going haywire."

"Quake sensors?" I asked.

"THEY DETECT GROUND MOVEMENT, MA'AM," he continued, "AND RIGHT NOW THEY'RE TELLING ME THAT THE GROUND BENEATH US IS HIGHLY UNSTABLE!"

"Wait a minute, Gax," I said, putting my hands on the walls around us. "I can feel it too!" There was only a slight vibration, but it was getting stronger and stronger.

"Spuckler!" I said, giving him a good shake. "Wake up!"

"Nguh?" Spuckler sputtered as he got up on his elbows. He was still half asleep, I thought.

"This snake is *moving!*" I told him. "Can you feel it?"

"Moving?" he repeated, rubbing his eyes.

"Mr. Beeba!" I said, rocking Mr. Beeba back and forth by the shoulders. He was still sound asleep, though, and showed no signs of waking up.

"Hey, you're right," Spuckler said, "she *is* sorta shakin' around a little, ain't she?" By then the movements were becoming more and more obvious.

"Mr. Beeba!" I said, shaking him as hard as I could.

"Here, 'Kiko, lemme help you out there," Spuckler said, crawling over to where Mr. Beeba was. Before I could stop him, Spuckler hauled off and smacked Mr. Beeba with his hand, good and hard, right on the side of his head.

"Aaughf!" Mr. Beeba groaned as he struggled to his feet.

"Look alive, Beebs," Spuckler said calmly. "The snake's startin' to fidget."

"You idiot!" Mr. Beeba shouted, now fully awake and very angry. "Don't you know any *civilized* ways of rousing a fellow from slumber?"

"Worked," Spuckler said with a shrug, "didn't it?"

By then the snake's movements had become impossible to ignore.

"My word!" Mr. Beeba whispered in alarm. "She *is* moving, isn't she?"

"She ain't just movin'," Spuckler shouted as there was a sudden lurch. "She's goin' *vertical* on us!"

Spuckler was right. It was like we were standing in the middle of a big long tube and someone was slowly raising it on one end, bit by bit. Before long what used to look like the floor was beginning to look like a wall, and we all started slipping and sliding down into the darkness. Meanwhile, Gax's torch was flickering all over the place, making it even harder to see straight.

"Heavens!" Mr. Beeba cried. "We'd better grab *on* to something!"

"B-but . . . ," I stammered, starting to panic, "there's nothing to grab on *to!*"

Everything was so slimy and slippery that it was

almost impossible to stop myself from sliding. By then the snake was almost completely vertical!

Luckily, Mr. Beeba was only about ten yards below me, and he was doing a much better job of holding on to the slimy walls. In fact, he was actually climbing up to help stop me from sliding any more.

"Just stay put, 'Kiko!" Spuckler called from above. "Beeba's gonna save ya!"

"It's too slippery!" I grunted as I slid down another few feet. By then Mr. Beeba was just a couple of yards below me.

"Hang on, Akiko!" he called desperately. "I'm almost there!"

"I'm losing my grip!" I cried as I felt myself begin to fall.

"Akiko!" Mr. Beeba shouted.

Just as I fell past him he reached out and grabbed my arm, squeezing as tightly as he could. He managed to hold me there for a minute or two.

"Don't worry, Akiko," he said to me. "I've got you!"

He tried to keep a grip on me, but my hand was covered with slime from the walls of the snake creature,

and I watched in horror as his fingers slowly slid
upward along my forearm. Before long it was just my
hand in his, and finally just the tips of my fingers all
scrunched up inside his fist.

"I can't . . . ," I gasped, "I can't hold on much longer!"

"But you *must*, Akiko!" Mr. Beeba cried desperately. "If you let go now you'll fall straight into the snake's stomach!"

Just as he said these words, my fingers slipped out of his. Giving a terrified shriek, I felt myself drop like a stone into the darkness below!

Chapter 8

I don't even like to *think* about what happened next, much less describe it in detail. Let's just say I was saved by a bad case of snake indigestion. Just as I was falling into the shadowy stomach of the snake, there was this huge belching sound, as loud as thunder. I felt myself being lifted up by a warm (and *very* disgusting-smelling) blast of air. With that one deafening burp, the snake began forcing me all the way back up its throat! It was pitch-black and I couldn't see a thing. Still, I could feel myself rocketing up through one slimy passage after another, until finally I flew right through the snake's mouth and out into the open air.

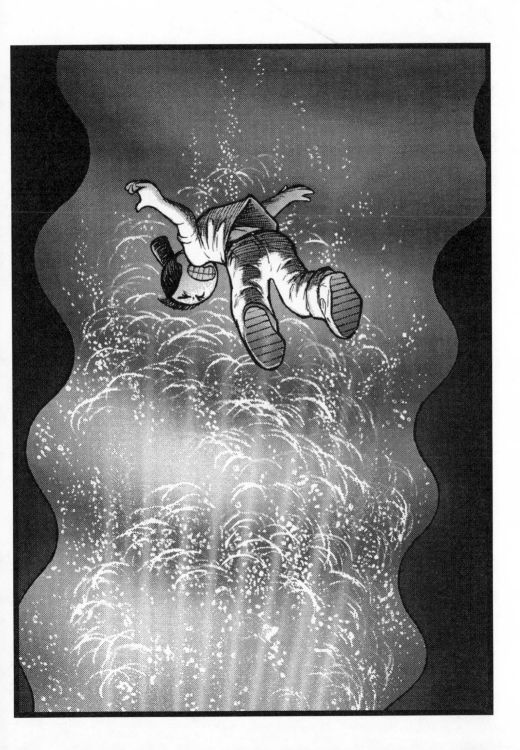

The next thing I knew, I was plunging down into the water of the Moonguzzit Sea. I was pretty dizzy, but luckily I was able to swim back to the surface and start treading water. It's a good thing my mom made me take those swimming classes at the YMCA when I was a kid!

There was a huge splash as the giant snake plunged back into the water. Its body rolled over and down until finally, with a flip of its long tail, it disappeared beneath the waves. I guess the old monster had lost its appetite.

Just when I was beginning to worry about whether the others had made it out alive, I heard voices from somewhere behind me: "Akikoooo!"

It was Spuckler, Mr. Beeba, Gax, and Poog. It turned out that they'd been carried up out of the snake just like I had been, and had landed a dozen or so yards away. They were all treading water and shouting at me over the waves.

"Thank *heavens* you're okay!" Mr. Beeba called out.

"You had us worried there for a minute, 'Kiko!" Spuckler shouted.

"That was, uh, kind of scary, wasn't it?" I answered breathlessly as I swam over to join them.

"We need to work on your vocabulary, Akiko," Mr. Beeba said disapprovingly. "The phrase 'kind of scary' doesn't capture it *at all*."

The sky was clear and sunny, and the water was pretty calm. As the waves carried us gently up and down, Spuckler started fiddling around with something inside Gax. He told us that Gax was equipped with a life raft, but he was having trouble getting it to inflate.

"This had better work, Spuckler," Mr. Beeba warned. "We can't tread water *indefinitely*, you know."

"Keep a lid on it, will ya, Beebs? I'm tryin' to concentrate here."

"JUST A LITTLE LOWER, SIR," Gax said, evidently enjoying himself. "YES, YES, THAT'S *MUCH* BETTER."

"This ain't a back rub, Gax," Spuckler said through clenched teeth. "*Release* the dang thing already, will ya?"

Finally there were several loud snapping sounds as a sheet of bright orange plastic shot out from underneath Gax, followed by a big whooshing noise as it began to fill with air. Within thirty seconds the raft was fully inflated and floating impressively on the surface of the water. It was pretty big, and I was relieved to see that there would be plenty of space for all of us.

"Climb aboard, everybody!" Spuckler said proudly as he helped us all into the raft. "The S.S. *Gax* is about to set sail!"

Chapter 9

We were all safely inside the raft, lazily drying ourselves off in the midday sun. After all we'd been
through, we definitely needed some time to recuperate.
Mr. Beeba, as always, was a little nervous about the possibility of something going wrong.

"Spuckler," he said, inspecting the well-worn surface
of Gax's raft, "are you sure this vessel is seaworthy?"

"Absolutely!" was Spuckler's confident reply. Then a
doubtful look came over his face. He turned to Gax
and asked, "Say, buddy, did I ever get around to
patchin' this thing?"

"NO, SIR," Gax answered bluntly.

"Aw, well, they ain't but tiny little holes anyway,"
Spuckler said after a pause. "We won't start sinkin' for
another *day* or two, I bet. . . ."

The thought of the raft having holes of any size was
not reassuring. Neither was the possibility of us floating around like this for days and days! I decided to see
if we couldn't speed things up a little.

"Mr. Beeba," I asked, "is there any limit to how high
up in the air Poog can fly?"

"I don't think so," he answered absentmindedly,
staring off across the waves. Spuckler busied himself

rearranging some of the pieces of equipment inside Gax's body.

"Well, then, maybe Poog can help us find the Sprubly Islands," I suggested.

There was a brief pause. Poog turned to face me.

"What are you getting at, Akiko?" Mr. Beeba asked, leaning forward with a puzzled expression.

"If Poog could fly up, way up into the air," I explained, "he might be able to see where the Sprubly Islands are. Then he could come back down and tell us what direction to go in and we could all paddle with our hands until we started heading in the right direction."

"Very clever," Mr. Beeba answered, sitting up straight. "Let's see if I can persuade Poog to take your plan into consideration."

But before Mr. Beeba could say another word, Poog began slowly floating up into the air. He rose higher and higher, like a child's lost balloon, until all we could see was a tiny purple speck against the sky hundreds of feet above us. Spuckler stopped working on Gax and looked up to see what Poog was doing.

"Astonishing!" Mr. Beeba said, shading his eyes with his hands as he followed Poog's progress. "I've never seen Poog act so quickly on a request like that. You've really got a *way* with him, Akiko."

"Really?" I asked, smiling. My face suddenly felt very warm, and I realized that I was blushing.

"Indeed," he answered, a hint of jealousy coming into his voice, "Poog doesn't often do the things *I* ask of him, and I've known him for a lot longer than you have!"

"It's, uh, probably just a coincidence," I said with a nervous chuckle.

"Oh no, Akiko," Mr. Beeba said with grave seriousness. "Mark my words: There's a special connection between you and Poog, one that I've seen developing from the moment you two met."

There was a long pause as I thought about Mr. Beeba's words. I looked up at the distant purple dot in the sky that was Poog and wondered what it meant to have a special connection to this strange floating alien. Somehow I sensed that there was more to it than Poog doing the things I asked of him. What would happen if Poog asked *me* to do something? Would I be able to do it?

A moment later Poog slowly floated back down to our raft. As usual it was hard to see much of an expression on his face, but I think I saw him smiling just a little. He turned to Mr. Beeba and blurted out a brief series of high-pitched syllables.

"Your scheme is a success, Akiko!" Mr. Beeba announced. "Poog has spotted the islands just a mile or two away, and the current is already carrying us in the right direction."

Spuckler let out a big whoop and I breathed a sigh of relief. Our luck was finally improving! We all started paddling like crazy, trying to get the raft to move as fast as possible. Before long my arms were very sore and I had to take a break. Mr. Beeba soon joined me, but Spuckler kept paddling for almost half an hour. Finally I began to see the silhouettes of trees on the horizon, hazy and blue in the late-afternoon sunlight.

"Everybody look over there!" I shouted, leaning over the edge of the raft and pointing frantically. "It's one of the Sprubly Islands!"

Chapter 10

Soon we were only half a mile or so from the shore. From what I could see, the beach appeared to be wide and sandy, with huge black boulders jutting out all over the place. As we floated closer, the raft got caught in a current that swiftly carried us toward land.

"Everybody hunker down, now," Spuckler warned. "If we hit one of them boulders, there's a good chance of gettin' knocked right outta the raft!"

I crouched low and braced myself as best I could, covering my head with my arms and drawing my legs under my body. Water sprayed over the edges of the raft and soaked us, just like on one of those water rides in an amusement park. The roar of the waves grew louder and louder as the raft rocketed past one black boulder and then another, until finally an enormous wave tossed the raft onto the beach, sending all of us sprawling headfirst onto the sand.

The water quickly receded into the sea, and we scrambled across the sand to avoid the next wave already sweeping in behind us. Spuckler picked both Gax and the raft up in his arms and carried them to a dry, sandy area far from the tide line. Mr. Beeba, his face covered in sand, stumbled after them and finally collapsed in exhaustion. Poog floated along to join them, and I walked unsteadily after Poog, my feet somehow unused to the feel of dry land.

We all sat down on the beach to catch our breath for a moment. Gax clicked and buzzed as he deflated the raft, carefully folded it up, and placed it in a compartment somewhere deep inside his body. Poog was humming quietly a few feet away from me, gazing out at the sea. I sat there on the sand, my elbows on my knees,

watching the waves roll in one after the other. The late-afternoon sun lit the beach from a very low angle, casting long thin shadows from every stone and seashell. A bunch of tiny crablike creatures skittered along a few yards from where I was sitting and a warm, soothing wind blew across my back. I could have sat that way for the rest of the day, except for one thing: My stomach was almost completely empty.

"I'm hungry," I said to no one in particular.

"You ain't the only one," Spuckler said, turning his head toward the forest behind us. "I wonder if there's anything eatable around here."

"*Edible*, Spuckler," Mr. Beeba instructed. "Edible."

"All right," I said decisively. "We've already achieved one of our goals: We've arrived safely in the Sprubly Islands. The next thing we have to do is find Queen Pwip."

"Agreed," Mr. Beeba said, as if he were checking things off a list in his head.

"But we're not going to find Queen Pwip tonight," I continued. "It's almost sundown, and besides, we're all half starved."

"So what's your plan, 'Kiko?" Spuckler asked, knocking his head with an open hand to dislodge some water from his ear.

"I say we go into this forest and see if we can find anything eatable," I answered. "I mean, *edible*."

"Good thinking, Akiko," Mr. Beeba said. "But we'd

better get moving. We only have a few minutes of sunlight left."

So we got to our feet and made our way up the beach and through the tall grasses that grew at the edge of the forest. The sun had nearly set, and the light gave the trunks of the trees a red-and-orange glow. Spuckler took the lead and we all followed obediently behind him. The forest was strangely quiet, apart from the occasional call of a bird high above.

As we went along, Mr. Beeba pointed out a number of plants he recognized from his studies in botany. He kept trying to make us memorize the names, like some overenthusiastic schoolteacher. Unfortunately, Spuckler and I were way too hungry to be appreciative students.

"Can anyone spot the coniferous twump?" Mr. Beeba asked as we lumbered farther into the increasingly dark woods. "Come on, now. I've pointed it out several times already."

"Beeba," Spuckler answered, "we don't want to hear about no more of your highfalutin plants. Not unless it's somethin' we can *eat*."

"Well, you wouldn't want to eat a coniferous twump," Mr. Beeba answered, a troubled expression coming over his face. "It's been known to make people's intestines explode!"

"We sure are hungry, Mr. Beeba," I said, trying not to imagine what it would feel like to have my intestines explode. "Aren't *any* of these plants safe to eat?"

"I appreciate your desire for a good square meal, Akiko, but you can't go through the forest eating things willy-nilly," Mr. Beeba answered, reaching out and grabbing hold of a small, smooth-surfaced fruit hanging from a nearby plant. "Take *this* fruit, for example: plump, fragrant, and pleasing to the eye; one might think it would make a *delightful* snack. . . ."

"That's all I need to hear," Spuckler said, snatching the fruit out of Mr. Beeba's hands and twisting it free from its stem.

"Spuckler! Wait!" Mr. Beeba pleaded. "I know *nothing* about this plant! It might upset your stomach! It . . . It could be poisonous!"

But it was too late. Spuckler ate the entire thing in a

couple of bites and swallowed with an audible gulp. There was a long, frightening pause as we watched to see what would happen. Gax made a squeaky churning sound as he raised his head to get a closer look at Spuckler's face. Poog hovered near Spuckler's shoulder, a slightly nervous expression in his eyes. Then Spuckler let out a loud belch and chuckled happily.

"These things are *good!*" Spuckler declared triumphantly, quickly plucking another one and tossing it in my direction. "Here, 'Kiko. Try one!"

I caught the little fruit with both hands and raised it to my face, slowly turning it over and inhaling its faintly sweet aroma. It was about the same size and texture as an eggplant, but its skin was dark blue with light blue spots, like some kind of exotic butterfly.

I knew that it was wrong to eat something out in the forest without being sure what it was. There was always the possibility that I'd end up getting a bad stomach-ache or even worse. Still, I was so hungry and the fruit smelled so good that I finally couldn't resist. I took a tiny little bite, chewed, and swallowed.

"Mmmm, they *are* good!" I said, taking another bite. It was a lot like a peach, except it tasted a little like strawberries, too. It was soft and juicy and had just one seed in the middle about the size of an almond. I went over and helped Spuckler find some more.

"Try one, Mr. Beeba," I said, handing him a smaller one I'd just picked. "It's better than staying hungry, trust me!"

"Well . . . ," Mr. Beeba replied, his resistance wearing down, "it *does* have a rather pleasant aroma. . . ."

After inspecting it thoroughly and wiping it vigor-ously against his clothes like a boy polishing an apple, Mr. Beeba took a bite of the mysterious blue-spotted fruit. Spuckler and I watched him as he slowly chewed and chewed and chewed. Finally he swallowed loudly and wiped the juice from his chin.

"Oh my," he said quietly, opening his eyes wide and licking his lips. "It *is* good, isn't it?"

Spuckler gave me a wink as if to say "I knew it!"

"Let's pick as many of them as we can!" Mr. Beeba said excitedly, no longer sounding the least bit cautious. "We've got to hurry! The daylight's almost gone!"

He was right. The forest was growing darker and darker, and now only the very tops of the trees were lit with a faint red-and-orange glow. Spuckler, Mr. Beeba, and I picked as many pieces of the fruit as we could and began placing them on the ground in little piles. Even Gax helped out a little, though as a robot he wouldn't end up eating any of them. Finally we all sat down on the ground and began our feast.

We laughed and joked with one another as we
stuffed ourselves with the fruit, smiling and spitting the
seeds in all directions. Mr. Beeba turned out to have
even more of an appetite than Spuckler and me put
together. By the time I had reached my limit, Mr. Beeba
had eaten more than two dozen pieces of the fruit and
showed no sign of slowing down.

"Beeba, take a *breather* for a second, will ya?" Spuckler
said, chuckling. "You're gonna make yourself sick!"

"You're quite right, Spuckler," Mr. Beeba replied,
grabbing another piece of fruit from the pile in front of
him. "I'll stop just as soon as I finish this stack."

It was right around then that I started to get this odd feeling all over my body. At first I thought I was getting an upset stomach, except I didn't feel really bad, just really . . . well, *weird*. It was like my whole body felt a little lighter or something. I looked over at Spuckler and noticed that he had a puzzled expression on his face.

"Hey, Beebs," he said, "ya really better stop eatin' that stuff, and I mean pronto. I'm startin' to feel a little . . . strange."

"I don't know what you're talking about, Spuckler," Mr. Beeba said between mouthfuls. "I've never felt better in my life."

Suddenly I had the odd sensation that I couldn't feel the ground underneath me anymore. I reached down to touch the ground and felt myself slowly float up into the air an inch or two!

"Whoah!" I gasped. "I'm . . . I'm *floating*, guys!"

I looked over and saw that Spuckler was no longer touching the ground either. In fact, he was hovering about six inches above it!

"Lordy!" he called out, laughing nervously. "So am I!

I'm sittin' on thin air!" Gax buzzed and whirred as he watched his master slowly float farther and farther away from the ground.

By that time Mr. Beeba had also started to rise into the air. Though normally I would have expected him to be in a panic, he was actually giggling and chuckling like a little child.

"Astounding!" he cried, beaming as he turned himself over in the air. "It must be something in the fruit! It's causing us to defy the law of gravity!"

I floated about two feet off the ground before leveling off, just bobbing up and down in the air like a duck on a pond. Spuckler rose about four feet before stopping and floating there in pretty much the same way. But Mr. Beeba was already nearly six feet off the ground and continued to float steadily upward with no sign of stopping. Rather than trying to slow himself down, he began flapping his arms around and swimming through the air as fast as he could. He was obviously enjoying himself.

"I'm soaring to the treetops!" he cried as he hurled himself into the air like a rocket. By the time he stopped he was at least forty feet above us, swimming in wide circles through the branches of the trees.

"Hey, Beeba, take it easy!" Spuckler shouted. "You ate too many of them things!"

"Yes, Mr. Beeba," I cried. "Come back down! It's too dark for you to see up there."

"Don't be silly!" Mr. Beeba called to us as he flew from one tree to another. "It's exhilarating up here! You two really ought to give it a try!"

"Beeba, I ain't kiddin'!" Spuckler yelled, his voice

growing angrier. "You're gonna get yourself killed!" It was odd and somehow very frightening to see Mr. Beeba acting so recklessly. It wasn't like him at all.

"Oh, listen to you!" Mr. Beeba laughed, flipping through the air like a trapeze artist. "For once I'm having a good time, and now suddenly you're crying out for prudence and caution! If I didn't know better, I'd think you were jealous!"

"'Kiko," Spuckler whispered, turning to me, "who *is* that guy up there, and what's he done with the real Beeba?"

"I know what you mean, Spuckler," I said. "He's kind of lost his mind, hasn't he?" We both strained to make out Beeba's silhouette against the ever-darkening sky. By that point he must have been seventy or eighty feet above us.

"Akiko! Spuckler!" we heard Mr. Beeba shout. "There's some kind of *animal* up here! I can hear him breathing!"

"Stay away, Beebs!" Spuckler cried, now very agitated. "You're probably invading his turf!"

Mr. Beeba pulled himself through the trees by grasping first one branch, then another, apparently trying to get a better look at the creature.

"Don't worry, little fellow," we heard Mr. Beeba say in a singsong voice. "I mean you no harm."

Just then there was a rustling from the trees, followed by a deep, rumbling growl. It sounded like a lion or something!

"*Beeba!*" Spuckler shouted as loudly as he could.

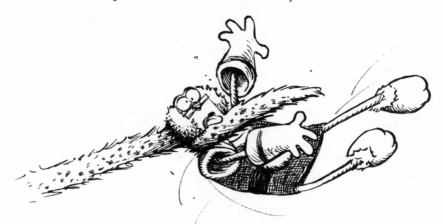

There was the sound of a brief struggle as twigs snapped and branches shook. Then the rustling grew quieter and quieter as it moved higher and higher into the trees.

A handful of leaves drifted slowly down from above.

A bird called out from somewhere far away.

Then it was completely quiet.

"*BEEBA!*" Spuckler howled, his voice echoing in the silence.

Spuckler and I, still floating just a few feet off the ground, stared at each other in shock as we realized Mr. Beeba was gone. Poog frowned and Gax made a long wheezing noise. Our little gang had just gone from five members to four!

"*You idiot!*" Spuckler shouted up at the trees, clenching his fists and spinning in circles. "I *told* you not to go up there!"

"What are we going to do?" I asked, suddenly feeling very scared.

"There's only one thing we *can* do!" Spuckler exclaimed, grabbing a piece of fruit from one of the piles beneath him. "I'm gonna eat some more of this stuff and go up there after him!"

"No, Spuckler!" I cried, my voice trembling. "Don't go! Don't leave me alone down here!" Stars were already visible through the trees, and it was starting to feel damp and chilly.

"Take it easy, 'Kiko," Spuckler said between mouthfuls as he swallowed one piece of fruit after another. "You ain't gonna be alone. Ya got Gax an' Poog here to keep ya company!"

Spuckler swallowed five or six more pieces of the fruit, then began floating up into the treetops.

"Don't worry, 'Kiko!" he called down to me before disappearing into the dark. "I'll be back with Beeba before ya know it!"

Chapter 12

The forest grew very quiet except for the steady chirping of insects in the bushes. Gax stretched his neck and watched the trees above us, as if already waiting for Spuckler to return. Poog just floated there in the darkness, his eyes blinking every so often, his face almost expressionless.

Gradually the effect of the fruit began to wear off, and I slowly floated back down. First one foot touched the ground, then the other, and a moment later I was sitting down just like I had been before. I crossed my arms in front of me, trying to keep warm. Having spent most of the journey with Spuckler and Mr. Beeba at my side, I suddenly felt frightened and very alone. I thought maybe I could take my mind off things by starting a conversation.

"I don't know how you can float around like that all day, Poog," I said, coughing and rubbing my hands together. "I started feeling kind of queasy after just a few minutes." Poog just smiled and blinked some more. The conversation was already over. I sat there a little longer in the darkness, trying to think of something that would help the situation.

There was a hooting somewhere up above, followed by the snapping of a twig just a few feet behind me. I spun my head around, half expecting to see some terrible hairy creature staring back at me. My heart was beating like a rabbit's, and I felt the hairs stand up on the back of my neck.

There was nothing there but bushes and tree trunks.

I looked around at Gax and Poog and gradually became more and more aware of how completely alone we were. I tried my best to stay calm, but panicky questions kept creeping into my mind. What if that strange creature had really *hurt* Mr. Beeba? What if Spuckler got lost? What if the creature had already defeated both Spuckler *and* Mr. Beeba and was coming back to . . .

I stopped myself from finishing that thought.

There was another hooting sound. Then a distant howl, like some strange sort of wolf. I suddenly had this very clear image in my mind of a gigantic, lizardy-looking animal with glowing red eyes, prowling around somewhere out there in the forest. I was so scared I was shaking all over, and I almost felt like I was going to cry.

"Spuckler," I said to myself, my voice sounding very shaky and scared, "you have *got* to get back here soon. I can't spend the night out here all alone. I'm not going to sleep a wink!"

Fortunately it got pretty quiet over the next ten minutes or so, and I managed to relax a little, even though I was still very nervous.

For some reason I started to think about a camping trip I went on with my parents back when I was about five years old. We went to a little campsite out in the

woods, in the middle of September after the real camping season was over. My favorite part was when my dad
built a fire at night. It helped keep us all warm, of
course, but it also made it a lot less scary to be out
there in the woods.

"That's it!" I said, turning excitedly to Gax. "We
need to build a campfire!"

"A CAMPFIRE?" Gax asked, cocking his head.

"Yeah. All we need to do is get some pieces of wood,
put them in a pile, and then . . ." It suddenly occurred
to me that I didn't have any matches.

". . . AND THEN?" Gax asked.

I sat there in the darkness looking at Gax and then at
Poog and then at Gax again. I remembered my science
teacher saying you could start a fire by rubbing two
sticks together, but every time I'd tried that all I'd ended
up with was a couple of warm sticks. There had to be
another way.

"Gax," I asked, "you've got a torch somewhere there
inside you, don't you?"

"YES, MA'AM," he answered, his robotic voice sounding very odd among the chirping of the insects, "BUT

I'M UNABLE TO OPERATE IT WITHOUT SPUCKLER'S
ASSISTANCE."

"Well, maybe *I* can figure it out," I said, refusing to
give up on the idea. "What does Spuckler usually do to
turn the thing on?"

"THERE'S A BUTTON ON THE SIDE OF MY BODY,"
Gax explained. "IT TURNS THE TORCH ON AND OFF."

I looked at the side of Gax's rusty, beat-up body.
There was a button there, all right—about *twenty* of
them! They were all laid out in neat little rows on a
small rectangular panel.

"Which one of these is for the torch?"

"I'M AFRAID I DON'T KNOW, MA'AM," Gax said
apologetically. "SPUCKLER GENERALLY JUST KEEPS PUSH-
ING BUTTONS UNTIL HE GETS WHAT HE WANTS."

"I see," I whispered, staring at all the buttons and
trying to detect some difference among them. It was
already so dark, though, that I could hardly see *anything*.

"Let's try this one," I said, pushing a button in the
lower left-hand corner of the panel.

SPROING!

A little door in Gax's side popped open and out

came a long metallic arm with a set of tools at the end: a hammer, a wrench, and a tiny little screwdriver.

"Wow. Cool!" I said. "But that's not what we're looking for, is it?"

I pressed another button.

BROING! FROING!

Immediately the little tool set drew back and folded out of sight. At the same time another door opened on the opposite side of Gax's body and a weird mechanical extension popped out with tubes at the end like some kind of plastic octopus.

"I wonder what *that's* for."

I kept pushing buttons.

TLUNK!

Things kept popping out. There was something that looked like an old-fashioned camera . . .

SPUP! BWANG!

. . . A boxing glove . . . a

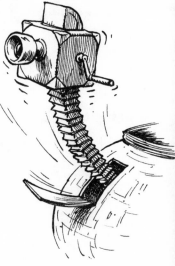

bottle of window spray . . .

GRONK! FRING!

. . . A bicycle horn . . . a shiny metallic toaster . . .

"YOU'RE *ENJOYING* THIS, *AREN'T* YOU?" Gax finally asked, a note of irritation in his crackly mechanical voice.

"I'm doing the best I can, Gax, honestly," I answered. He was right, though. It *was* kind of fun, I had to admit!

FRAAAAW!

Finally I pushed the right button and Gax's torch sprang out: a blindingly bright white flame flickering at the end of a long mechanical arm. I had to turn my face away for a minute while my eyes adjusted to the light. Suddenly all the tree trunks around us were brightly lit and even very distant trees became clearly visible. A couple of mothlike bugs immediately fluttered in and began circling Gax's flame.

"All right, Gax! Hang on a minute, now," I said excitedly as I cleared a spot on the ground. I didn't want to take any chances of starting a forest fire, so I cleared a nice big area and surrounded it with stones. Then I made a little pile of dry wood in the middle of the stones. I took a long stick over to Gax's torch and set it aflame, then brought the burning stick over to the pile of wood. It took a minute or two, but slowly the dry pieces of wood lit up, and before long we had a nice little campfire.

Gax extinguished his torch, carefully folding it up and stowing it inside his body. Poog hovered near my shoulder, the bright flames of the fire perfectly mirrored in his big, glassy eyes. I leaned back on my elbows and watched the flames jump back and forth.

There was no sound at all except for the quiet chirping of the forest insects and the crackle of the campfire.

"How long do you think it'll be before they come back, Gax?" I asked.

"IT'S HARD TO SAY, MA'AM. SOMETIMES SPUCKLER IS GONE FOR *WEEKS*," he answered. That's the problem with robots. They always tell you the truth, even when you'd rather they didn't.

"Well, he told us to stay here, so that's exactly what we're going to do," I said, doing my best to sound determined and unafraid. "We're going to sit right here and . . ."

I felt a yawn coming on.

". . . and . . ."

I stretched my mouth open and let out one of the biggest, longest yawns I can remember. Even Poog looked a little surprised!

"Boy, I'm beat!" I said, rubbing my eyes with both hands. "Gax, would you mind keeping watch while I take a little nap?"

"NOT AT ALL, MA'AM," he answered, raising his head into a position of complete alertness. "IT WOULD BE MY PLEASURE."

I gathered a bunch of leaves to use as a pillow and flopped over on my side, turning my back to the warmth of the fire.

I started to think about Queen Pwip. I wondered what she looked like. Was she was friendly? Did she wear fancy clothes and live in a big palace? I wondered if she really could see the future, and if so, how she did it. Did she use a crystal ball, or just close her eyes and concentrate really hard?

Then I started to think about my parents again. I remembered that camping trip and how we all slept together in a tent every night. My parents seemed like they were having a ball, but I wasn't too crazy about the whole experience. It was awfully cold at night, and even during the day it still wasn't warm enough to go swimming, so there really wasn't much of anything to do. Then there was the food! My mom and dad kept telling me how great it was to eat fresh salmon that had been grilled over the fire, but I thought it just tasted like burned, salty fish.

Now, though, it all seemed like a very happy memory. I suddenly wished I could be with my parents again, just for a minute or two, so I could talk to them and be sure they were okay.

I rolled over onto my back and opened my eyes again. I stared up past the treetops into the starry sky and wondered if one of those stars wasn't really the planet Earth. Maybe I was so far from Earth that it looked just like a tiny point of light up in the sky. . . .

Chapter 13

In the middle of the night I woke up. The fire had died down a little but it was still quite warm. Gax was slowly turning his head back and forth as he kept watch over us. The sound of the insects seemed much louder than it had before. There was still no sign of Mr. Beeba or Spuckler.

Then I noticed Poog staring at me. He had floated over until he was just a foot or two from my face. I could see my own groggy expression reflected in his big black eyes. He had this very serious look on his face, one I was sure I'd never seen before.

"What is it, Poog?" I asked, sitting up. "Are you okay?"

Poog opened his mouth and said something in that weird warbly language of his. It was only about a second or two long, but seemed to be made up of eight or nine syllables. He said it again.

"I'm sorry, Poog," I said, wishing Mr. Beeba were there to translate. "I don't understand."

But he kept saying this thing to me, this same short little alien phrase, like it was very, very important. He must have repeated it about ten times. Slowly I realized what Poog was trying to do. He was *teaching* me the words. He wanted me to listen to them and repeat them.

So I tried. I listened as best I could to the little phrase, but it was very hard to repeat the whole thing. I decided just to start with the first couple of syllables and try to learn it a little at a time. I guess Poog knew what I was trying to do, because he broke the phrase down and gave it to me in little pieces. There were some sounds that required sticking my tongue up against the roof of my mouth in a very uncomfortable way. There were also a couple of clicking sounds that reminded me of an African language I'd heard on television once. It was so difficult to pronounce, I really didn't think I'd be able to do it. I could tell by the way Poog would sort of

wince every once in a while that my pronunciation was pretty awful.

But he wouldn't give up. He kept repeating the phrase, the first part of it, the second part of it, and the last part of it. Finally I said it once all the way through from beginning to end. Poog smiled. I got it wrong again once or twice after that, but then I said it right again, and eventually I started saying it right more often than saying it wrong. He made me practice it twenty or thirty times, until finally I was able to say it pretty quickly. When Poog seemed satisfied that I had memorized the phrase, he smiled and closed his eyes. Then he floated back until he was a couple of yards away from me and began humming quietly to himself. I watched him for a minute or so, but soon I put my head back down and closed my eyes too. A moment later I was fast asleep again.

Chapter 14

The next sound I heard was a little voice right next to my face.

"Just as I suspected," the voice said. "She's dead."

I opened my eyes. It was morning, and a soft yellow light covered the ground in front of me. There, an inch or two from my nose, stood the tiniest little man imaginable. He was no taller than two or three inches from head to toe! He was dressed in military uniform, with an oversized helmet and big clumsy boots. His back was turned to me, and I realized that he was not alone. Two or three feet before him stood an entire *army* of little soldiers just as small as he was. There were hundreds of them, standing at attention in neat little rows!

I lifted my head from the ground and they all jumped back in fear. The little man in front of my face, who I figured was their leader, whirled around and looked me in the eye. His mouth dropped open and his knees seemed to buckle underneath him.

"She's not dead!" he sputtered. "Sh-she's moving!"

He drew a miniature sword from a sheath at his side, held it high in the air, and spun around to address his army at the top of his voice.

"Troops!" he bellowed. "Take your positions!"

I sat up and watched in amazement as the army divided itself into three perfectly equal groups and marched left, right, and center to form an impressive arc around me. They all carried tiny swords and shields and were dressed in suits of gray-and-black armor. I could tell by their speed and precision that they had practiced this sort of maneuver many times before.

"Quickly! Quickly!" their leader shouted. "Remember your training!"

"I must be dreaming," I whispered to myself, rubbing my eyes and trying to convince myself this wasn't really happening.

BLAAAAAAAAAT!

The sound of a tiny trumpet pierced the air, and the soldiers all stopped and stood at attention. The silence that followed was somehow even more frightening than all the commotion that had preceded it.

"Prepare your weapons!" the leader shouted as it slowly dawned on me what they were preparing to do. "Attack the intruder!"

"Wait!" I shouted, raising my hands into the air. The men grimaced and some of them covered their ears. I realized that my voice must sound incredibly loud when heard by ears as small as theirs.

"Please stop!" I said in a quieter voice, raising my hands even higher. "I surrender!"

"Halt!" the commander ordered, even though none of the soldiers had actually started to attack. I'm pretty sure they were just as scared of me as I was of them. I remember my mom once telling me that bees only sting people when they get scared and they have to defend themselves. I think these soldiers were probably a lot like that: not mean or anything, just awfully frightened.

The leader guy turned once again to face me, and for the first time I got a good look at him. He had a big, bushy mustache and a shiny little monocle over one eye. His head was wider at the bottom than it was at the top, mainly because of his oversized jaw.

"Surrender, eh?" he said with a stern expression, as if he didn't quite believe me. Then he slowly relaxed and a smile came over his face.

"I salute your good sense!" he cheerfully declared, replacing his sword in its sheath. "You're *bigger* than we are, obviously, but we've got you *outnumbered*, haven't we?"

"Men," he shouted over his shoulder, "sheathe your

swords!" There was a clattering as all the soldiers put their swords away. I'd swear I heard some of the soldiers breathe a sigh of relief.

"As you can see," the commander continued, pointing to something behind me, "your accomplices have also given up without a fight." I turned my head to find Gax and Poog similarly surrounded by hundreds of tiny armed soldiers. Gax had a confused look on his face, but Poog seemed calm.

"Who . . . ," I began, my voice still a little rough from sleep, ". . . who *are* you?"

"Silence!" the commander bellowed, pointing an accusing finger at me. "*I* ask the questions! *You* give the answers!"

He glared at me for a moment, then continued in a much quieter voice: "But since you've asked . . ."

He put one hand on his hip and thrust his chest forward proudly.

". . . I am Admiral Frutz, special advisor to Her Majesty Queen Pwip!"

Chapter 15

Queen Pwip! I couldn't believe it. Suddenly I was very glad to see this little man, and extremely curious as to whether Queen Pwip was just as small as he was. It was hard for me to imagine that "Her Majesty" was only a few inches tall! Still, Poog had said she'd be able to help us, so I guess it didn't really matter *what* size she was.

"You work for Queen Pwip?" I asked excitedly.

"*Silence!*" Admiral Frutz shouted, pointing another accusing finger at me. "You are not worthy to speak her name!"

"Sorry," I said, and kept quiet. I could tell the best

way to get along with this guy was to let *him* do all the talking.

Admiral Frutz opened a decorative canister attached to his belt and pulled out a tightly rolled piece of paper tied with a bright golden ribbon. He made an elaborate show of removing the ribbon and unrolling the scroll from top to bottom. Then he cleared his throat and began reading from it in a very formal tone.

"'A Royal Decree from Her Majesty Queen Pwip!'" he shouted. A reverent hush fell over the already quiet troops. Poog, Gax, and I tried to remain absolutely still.

"'In her infinite mercy, Her Majesty hereby orders that the *foul intruders*,'" he announced, staring at me as if to make sure I realized whom he was talking about, "'are to be spared any bodily harm.'" I breathed a sigh of relief and he glared angrily at me for a moment before returning to the Royal Decree.

"'Instead, Admiral Frutz and the SIRAR . . .'" He stopped briefly to explain. "That's the Sprubly Islands Royal Army and Reserve, mind you. It's an acronym." He cleared his throat again, taking a moment to find the spot where he had left off.

"'Admiral Frutz and the SIRAR,'" he began again, "'are to escort the trespassers back to Queen Pwip's palace for her personal interrogation. There they will be detained until such time as Her Majesty deems it fitting and proper that they be granted freedom. Her Majesty has spoken!'" He made a quick little bow before rolling up the scroll and carefully replacing it in its container.

I glanced quickly at Poog, who was smiling peacefully as if this were all part of some plan he had. I wish I could have been so calm about things. All I could do was think about how I'd promised that we'd stay right there in that same spot until Spuckler returned with Mr. Beeba. What if they came back and found us gone? They'd probably think we'd panicked and abandoned them or something. The possibility of the five of us becoming permanently separated was almost too scary to consider. I figured I had to at least *try* to delay our departure as long as possible.

"Look, uh, Mr. Frutz—" I began.

"It's *Admiral* Frutz, you meatheaded monstrosity!" he bellowed, stabbing one of his little arms into the air. "And besides, I have *not* given you permission to speak!"

There was a long pause as Admiral Frutz turned to face his men, who had stood obediently at attention the entire time. He raised his sword as if he were about to call out a new order, then stopped, replaced the sword at his side, and slowly turned to face me again.

Oh, all right, what *is* it, then?" he asked with an exasperated sigh.

"Couldn't we stay here just a *little* bit longer?" I pleaded. "I promised my friends that I wouldn't leave until they came back."

"What do you think I am? A *baby-sitter?*" he shouted angrily. "I will allow *no* such delays!" He spun around, raised his sword, and called out to his troops.

"Prisoner Escort Formations! Right! Left! Center!"

The troops swarmed around us into an entirely new series of rows and columns, all facing in one direction. Suddenly I felt like Gax, Poog, and I were giant floats in a miniature Thanksgiving Day parade, with all the men ready to march us down the middle of Main Street. There was no real street, of course. But looking carefully, I could see a narrow path running through the forest that had been entirely invisible the night before. The path was covered with millions and millions of tiny footprints from all the tiny soldiers.

"Prisoners!" Admiral Frutz shouted up at Poog, Gax, and me. "On your feet!"

I knew there was nothing I could say that would

change the admiral's mind, so I slowly stood up. There were a few muffled gasps from the soldiers as they became aware of my full height. I've never felt so tall in my entire life! It was like I was looking down at them from the top of a skyscraper or something.

A trumpet blast sounded and the soldiers began marching forward. They were so small, though, that they couldn't move very fast. I had to take little baby steps just to be sure I wouldn't leave them all behind or accidentally squash one of them like a little bug. I glanced back at Gax and Poog, who were quietly following me. Then I looked up into the trees, half hoping to see Spuckler and Mr. Beeba floating back down to rejoin us, but all I could see was the hazy morning sunlight coming through the leaves. I shuddered a little as I realized we might never see them again.

Chapter 16

Admiral Frutz's army marched us through the woods as fast as they could, which is to say, at a snail's pace. Eventually we came to a clearing in the trees. At that point the narrow path became a slightly wider dirt road, and the pace of the soldiers picked up just a little. On either side of the road were gently rolling hills covered with miniature grasses and wildflowers. Off to one side in the distance I could see the Moonguzzit Sea. The sun had risen higher in the morning sky, and some of the haze had burned off. One or two clouds dotted the sky, but otherwise there was nothing but blue as far as the eye could see.

"Will you *please* slow down?" Admiral Frutz shouted up at me, temporarily marching backward to glare at me from his position at the head of the procession. "My men's legs are *much* shorter than yours!" I had begun to outpace everyone and the entire army was almost sprinting to keep up with me.

"Sorry!" I said, going back to my baby steps. "Is Queen Pwip's palace very much farther?"

"Silence!" came Admiral Frutz's reply.

Eventually we began to pass evidence of people living nearby. There were tiny stone walls separating one property from another, and small plots of land with neat little rows of leafy vegetables. Then I spotted a miniature farmhouse, surrounded by a tiny wooden fence. The farther we walked, the more houses I saw, each surrounded by strips of farmland and pastures grazed by tiny barnyard animals. It was very weird being able to look down on it all from my point of view, kind of like walking and looking out an airplane window at the same time.

Finally the farmland began to give way to little villages and towns. Gax clicked and whirred as he rotated his head left and right to take it all in. I think he was

just as fascinated as I was. There were tiny cobblestone streets and open-air marketplaces, miniature chimneys spouting tiny puffs of smoke, and hundreds of little Sprublian men and women going about their tiny lives. Wherever we went people stopped and stared, pointing and whispering excitedly to one another. There were so many strange and wonderful sights, I wanted to stop and get a closer look at everything.

Admiral Frutz kept us marching, though, and by the looks of things Queen Pwip's palace wasn't very far away. For one thing, we now found ourselves marching through the hustle and bustle of a much bigger city. The road we were on had widened considerably and was decorated on both sides by elaborate street lamps and ornate little statues. The buildings were larger and more stately (though even the biggest came no higher than my waist), and there were beautiful parks and gardens on all sides. The city people were not easily impressed, though. They glanced up at us from their newspapers, squinted, and went back to their business.

Finally we came to the gates of the palace grounds. An enormous wall surrounded the complex, a beautifully detailed structure that stood about six feet high. There were elaborate turrets and guard towers, with domes that looked like they been plucked from an Arabian mosque. The entire surface of the wall was covered with polished yellow and turquoise stones that sparkled and shimmered in the morning sunlight. The road we were marching on led directly to a large gateway that was sealed by two ornate doors.

"Halt!" Admiral Frutz shouted. There was a trumpet blast from the rear of the procession, followed by a series of deeper notes sounded by trumpets inside the palace. A minute or two of silence passed as we waited for the gates to be opened.

Then slowly, almost without a noise, the doors parted. Before us, a series of wide stairways led up to a beautiful miniature palace. The whole thing was no more than seven or eight feet high, but it was just about the most amazing building I'd ever seen. It was made up of at least a dozen towers, each topped with an onion-shaped dome that glittered and sparkled like a piece of jewelry. There were elaborately decorated balconies, silvery-shuttered windows, and glistening urns overflowing with exotic plants and flowers. The building was surrounded by dozens of lanterns and incense burners, some embedded in the polished marble of the palace's foundation, others perched atop ornate golden pedestals.

I heard a muffled clattering sound as Admiral Frutz's soldiers dropped to their knees and bowed their heads.

Admiral Frutz marched forward through the gates and got a foot or so into the palace grounds before stopping and turning impatiently to me.

"Come on, then!" he said in a loud whisper. "And don't touch anything!"

Chapter 17

Gax, Poog, and I followed Admiral Frutz through the gates, leaving his army outside. As soon as we passed through them, the gates quietly closed behind us, shutting out all the sounds of the surrounding city. The only noises remaining were the squeak of Gax's wheels as he rolled along behind me, and the echoing clank of Admiral Frutz's boots as he marched up the tiny marble steps in front of us. When we got within a couple of feet of the palace, Admiral Frutz ordered us to stop.

"No *funny* business, now," he warned. "An audience with Queen Pwip is a very auspicious honor, and you are expected to behave accordingly." I wasn't even sure what the word *auspicious* meant, but I got the general idea of what Admiral Frutz wanted from me. I nodded solemnly and kept my mouth shut.

Admiral Frutz clicked his heels and marched into the palace through a side door. There was a minute or two of absolute silence as we stood there all alone. I took the opportunity to ask Poog a question.

"Poog," I whispered, "Queen Pwip isn't real *mean* or anything, is she?"

Poog just smiled and said nothing. It was hard to tell if he could understand anything I'd said. I suppose even if he *had* understood, there was no use in his answering me, since everything he said came out in that weird garbly language of his. I sighed and wished Mr. Beeba were still around. I started worrying about Spuckler and Mr. Beeba again but made myself think of something else.

Minute after minute passed, and still there was no sign of Queen Pwip. I turned around and started to examine a decorative little lamp just a foot or two behind me. It was built entirely out of a beautiful brass-colored metal and covered with decorative carvings. I ran my fingers over its surface and found it surprisingly cool to the touch.

"DO BE CAREFUL, MA'AM," Gax cautioned me. "THE ADMIRAL TOLD US NOT TO TOUCH ANYTHING."

"I know, Gax," I answered, leaning over to see my own reflection in the highly polished surface. "But it's all so *pretty*."

"It had *better* be pretty," said a tiny, high-pitched voice in reply, "what with all the trouble I had to go through to get this thing built!"

I spun around and looked every which way to see where the voice had come from.

"Over here, my child!" called the voice, and this time I realized that it was coming from inside the palace. My eyes darted around until finally I saw a tiny figure deep inside one of the balconies, half hidden in the shadows cast by the late-morning sun. The figure glided forward into the sunlight, revealing a beautiful little woman no taller than Admiral Frutz. She was dressed from head to toe in satiny white robes with blue embroidery, and wore a large round hat that made her head look even smaller than it was. Her eyes were shiny and black like two tiny drops of ink, and her hair was long and straight, falling over her shoulders and about halfway down her back. She wore a happy little smile on her lips that told me at once I had nothing to fear. I smiled back at her and she gave me a wink.

Admiral Frutz stepped forward from behind her, bowed, and spoke to me in a very stiff voice as if he was reciting something from memory.

"It is a profound honor and privilege to present to you the Greatest Monarch of this or any age, the Fairest Ruler ever to grace the surface of the Sprubly Islands, the Brightest Shining Beacon of virtue and beneficence ever to—"

"Frutz!" the woman interrupted impatiently. "Can't you *abbreviate* this introduction of yours? I'd swear it gets longer every time you do it."

"I, er . . . ," Admiral Frutz stammered, suddenly sounding very mild and harmless, "I'll see what I can do about it, Your Majesty." The woman stepped forward, motioning Admiral Frutz to one side.

"I'm Pwip," she said in a very casual voice, "Queen of the Sprubly Islands. Welcome to my palace, Akiko."

"H-how did you know my name?" I asked, genuinely startled. I'd never told Admiral Frutz, after all. Queen Pwip let out a pleasant little laugh.

"I know a great many things about you, Akiko," she said with a smile, "and about your friends here, Poog and Gax." Poog smiled and nodded, and Gax lifted his head higher with a brief series of electronic clicks.

"But that shouldn't surprise you," she continued. "Why, it's the only reason you've come looking for me, isn't it? To find out the things I know."

"Well, um, yes, that's true, I guess," I answered nervously. There was something unsettling about talking to a woman who knew so many things without having to be told. I suddenly realized there was nothing I could keep secret from her.

"That's nothing to worry about, though, dear child," she responded, as if she'd heard my thoughts loud and clear. "Why would you want to keep anything secret from me anyway?" She smiled warmly, and I began to feel a little less nervous.

"Your Majesty," Admiral Frutz whispered urgently. "Your kindness toward these prisoners is most generous, but we mustn't forget that they were caught in flagrant violation of the Antitrespassing Act of 1403. The stipulated punishment is beheading, is it not?"

"Frutz!" Queen Pwip said, raising her voice. "I know *quite* well what violations have taken place and the punishments that are stipulated. This matter is now under my jurisdiction. Why don't you run along and do some . . . I don't know, *drills* or something?"

"But, Your Majesty," Admiral Frutz protested, "I couldn't possibly leave you alone with these dangerous criminals."

"They are *not* criminals, Frutz," Queen Pwip explained wearily.

"But, Your Majesty—"

"Are you *disobeying my orders*, Frutz?" Queen Pwip asked, her face tightening into a threatening scowl.

"No, Your Majesty, I—I . . . ," Admiral Frutz
stammered nervously, "I . . ."

There was a heavy silence as Queen Pwip stared
Admiral Frutz down. Finally his little face loosened up
and his jaw dropped a few notches, leaving him looking
like a sad little puppy dog. He stared down at his shoes
and bowed obediently.

"I'll be just outside the gate, Your Majesty."

"*Thank* you," Queen Pwip said, sighing to herself before turning to face me again. She smiled and waited while Admiral Frutz retreated into the palace, his boots clinking and clattering as he marched across the polished marble floor.

"You'll have to forgive old Frutzy," she said at last, turning to me like an old friend. "He means well, really. But he *does* get a little overprotective at times, I'm afraid." I was pretty impressed with the way Queen Pwip had ordered Admiral Frutz around. She didn't look mean or tough at all, but she spoke in a way that made people listen to her.

"Come follow me, Akiko," she said, "and bring your friends. There are some people I think you should meet." I watched as she descended a spiral staircase off to one side of the balcony and reappeared just a foot or so from where I was standing. She was so small she barely came up to my ankle, but she didn't seem frightened of me in the least.

She showed us to a gateway in the back of the palace and began leading us into a whole new section of the palace grounds. Gax, Poog, and I followed close behind.

"Thank you, Queen Pwip," I said.

"Why, whatever for, dear child?" she asked with a laugh.

"For not, uh, *beheading* us or anything."

This produced an even louder laugh, and Queen Pwip dismissed my words with a wave of her hand.

"Akiko, my dear girl!" she said cheerfully as she turned a corner and led us beneath one final decorative arch. "No one has *ever* been beheaded in the Sprubly Islands! Admiral Frutz makes that sort of thing up just to impress his men."

Queen Pwip came to a stop before a large iron gate. It stood about six feet tall and barred the entrance to a walled courtyard filled with miniature trees, colorful gardens, and . . .

. . . Spuckler and Mr. Beeba!

I couldn't believe my eyes. There at the far side of the courtyard sat Spuckler and Mr. Beeba, leaning against a wall and resting in the sun. When they saw me looking in at them they scrambled to their feet.

"Akiko!" they both cried together, dashing across the courtyard as fast as they could.

Chapter 18

Queen Pwip smiled as we all chattered excitedly.

"Thank heavens they found you!" Mr. Beeba said.

"How ya doin' there, Gax?" Spuckler asked, stretching a hand through the bars of the gate to touch Gax's helmet.

"I'M STILL IN GOOD WORKING ORDER, SIR," Gax answered. "I DIDN'T FEEL QUITE MYSELF WITHOUT YOU, THOUGH."

"*Course* ya didn't!" Spuckler said proudly.

"But how did you guys *get* here?" I asked. "I thought you were still out in the forest somewhere."

"Yes, and we thought the very same thing about you,"

Mr. Beeba replied, scratching his head vigorously. "Your Majesty, perhaps some explanations are in order?"

"All in good time, friends, all in good time," Queen Pwip said. She then clapped her hands together twice quickly and made a high-pitched whistling sound through her teeth.

"Jorrah!" she cried as loudly as she could. "Come on, girl!"

A soft pattering noise echoed through the complex. It was a galloping sound, like some kind of animal. A fearful look came over Mr. Beeba's face, and Spuckler seemed to brace himself for a fight.

I turned my head to follow Mr. Beeba's gaze and saw a big spotted animal trotting in our direction. It looked something like a leopard and was around six feet long from the tip of its nose to the end of its tail. Its fur was yellow with gray spots, and its tail was two or three times longer than its entire body. It had big sharp teeth but somehow appeared very tame. Coming to a stop at Queen Pwip's side, the creature sat down and waited obediently.

"Stand back, Akiko!" Mr. Beeba shouted. "That beast is unstoppable! She uses that tail like a weapon!"

"Oh, calm down, Mr. Beeba," Queen Pwip said, stroking the animal's whiskers. "She's as gentle as can be, provided she doesn't see you as a threat.

"Now, Jorrah," Queen Pwip went on, directing the animal to face me, "I want you to meet Akiko."

The animal leaped forward with a jerk and gave my face a thorough licking with her big wet tongue. I tried

to turn away, but that was pretty much impossible, so I just gave in and tried to enjoy it. She reminded me a little of my uncle Koji's dog, John, who was just as affectionate (and smelled the same too).

"Heavens!" Mr. Beeba exclaimed. "I wish this beast had been so docile when she came across *me!*"

"No way!" I said. "*This* is the animal that attacked you in the forest last night?"

"The very one," Mr. Beeba answered ruefully. "She coiled that tail around me so tightly that I was scarcely able to breathe. Then she dragged me all the way back here to Queen Pwip's palace."

"She's a *fast* little critter too," Spuckler joined in. "I almost lost the trail a couple times tryin' to keep up!"

"I see," I said. "So *that's* how you both got here!"

"Yes," Queen Pwip explained. "You can imagine my surprise. Jorrah has been known to bring home the occasional forest animal, but never anything quite like *these* two." She laughed and turned to Spuckler and Mr. Beeba.

"I'm terribly sorry I had to keep you under palace arrest all night," she explained to them. "One never knows, though. Not all Big People are as civilized as you, I'm afraid." She pulled out an ornate silvery key and used it to open a lock at the very bottom of the gate. Spuckler pulled the gate open with a loud squeak.

"We certainly understand, Your Majesty," Mr. Beeba replied with a smile as he and Spuckler stepped out of their place of confinement. "I'm sure we'd have done the same thing had the circumstances been reversed."

"And I owe *you* an apology as well, Akiko," Queen Pwip said with an embarrassed smile. "When Mr. Beeba told me about you and your friends still out there in the forest, Admiral Frutz *insisted* that I let him capture you with his army. I felt rather sure that it wasn't necessary, but old Frutzy does so *love* to capture things. I hope he didn't frighten you."

"No, he didn't," I answered, grinning. "Well, not very *much*, anyway."

"You must let me make it up to you, Akiko," Queen Pwip announced decisively. "Please join me for tea."

"We would be *delighted* to, Your Majesty," Mr. Beeba answered excitedly. "Your generosity is most appreciated!"

"I wasn't inviting *you*, Mr. Beeba," Queen Pwip explained bluntly. Mr. Beeba's jaw dropped a little.

"If you don't mind," she continued, "I'd like to speak with Akiko and Poog in private." A weird feeling came over me. It was like being sent to the principal's office at school, except I was pretty sure I wasn't in trouble.

"B-but of course," Mr. Beeba stammered.

"In the meantime, perhaps you and Spuckler and Gax could do a bit of housecleaning for me."

"Housecleanin'?" Spuckler asked, rubbing his jaw doubtfully.

"Do you see those domes on the palace wall?" she asked, indicating dozens and dozens of golden structures all along the wall that surrounded the grounds. "They're terribly hard for my men to reach. By the time they've cleaned them from one end of the wall to the other, they have to start all over again from the beginning."

I followed the entire wall with my eyes, trying to imagine the hundreds of little men it would take to polish all those domes. Queen Pwip was right. Spuckler and Mr. Beeba would be able to do the job a lot faster, especially if Gax helped out.

"But, Your Majesty . . . ," Mr. Beeba began.

"No problem, Queen Pwip!" Spuckler announced cheerfully. "Jus' give us a handful of cleanin' rags and we'll go t' town on them suckers!"

"*Thank* you, Spuckler," Queen Pwip said with a smile, followed by a disapproving glance at Mr. Beeba. "I'll have Admiral Frutz supply you with everything you'll need." She clapped her hands and Jorrah jumped to her feet.

"Come along, then," Queen Pwip said to me and Poog. "The three of us have got quite a lot to talk about."

Chapter 19

After ordering Admiral Frutz to give Mr. Beeba and the others a large supply of cleaning materials, Queen Pwip led Poog and me to a different section of the grounds. After passing through a big decorative arch, we came to a small circular building with a wide stained-glass dome on top and a little round door in front. It stood in the center of a large circle of grass that had been allowed to grow high and uncut. The whole structure looked much older and more weather-beaten than the rest of the palace. There were lots of cracks in the walls, and the pale gold surface of the door looked like it would probably never shine again no matter how much anyone polished it.

"This is the oldest building in the Sprubly Islands," Queen Pwip said to me in a reverent tone. "It stood here long before this palace was built. It's called the Seeing Room. This is where I go to find out about all manner of things kept secret from me by time and space." She looked me up and down from head to toe, as if measuring me with her eyes.

"It's going to be a tight squeeze, but I think you'll *just* manage to fit inside."

She reached into her robes, pulled out a very old, rusty-looking key, and unlocked the ancient door with a loud creaking noise. She pulled the doors open as far as possible. Even then the doorway was only about two feet wide, and I felt a little like I was being asked to get inside a doghouse or something.

"Come on, now," Queen Pwip said with a grin. "Don't tell me you're afraid to get your hands dirty." I gave Poog a nervous look. He just smiled and nodded.

So I got down on my hands and knees and carefully crawled through the narrow passageway into the dimly lit room within. The first thing I noticed was how cool it was. The temperature must have been at least ten degrees lower than it was outside. The circular room was about six feet from one side to the other, and the ceiling was no more than four feet above the floor. I crawled to one side, trying as hard as I could not to bump my head on the ceiling. There was just enough space for me to sit crouched against the wall with my legs pulled up underneath me.

A pale purplish light filtered in through the stained-glass dome above, revealing tiny specks of dust drifting through the air. There was no furniture or object of any kind, except for a pool of water held in a round stone basin in the middle of the floor. The smell of incense hung in the air. There was something very—I don't know—*peaceful* about the place. It was as if any troubles you might have would just disappear as soon as you entered.

I sat and watched as Poog slowly floated in after me. He glided right into the center of the room, pausing for a moment to observe his reflection in the pool of water, then chose a spot in the air next to me and hovered there without making a sound.

Queen Pwip closed the doors behind her and walked to a spot opposite Poog and me, resting her hands on the rugged surface of the stone basin. She raised her eyes and gave me a very serious look for what seemed like a long time, then smiled and chuckled to herself. Then she stared into the water and said nothing at all for about five minutes. I probably should have just kept quiet, but my curiosity got the better of me.

"What's going on?" I asked. "What are you looking at?"

"Hush, Akiko," she answered gently. "There are no questions in the Seeing Room. Only answers."

She continued staring at the water, resting her hands on the edge of the basin without making the slightest movement. Then something very odd happened.

PLIP!

There was a little splash in the center of the pool, as if a single drop of water had fallen into it from above. I looked up into the stained-glass dome, thinking there

must have been some kind of leak.
I stared at the glass, trying hard
to keep my eyes wide open.

PLIP!

This time I
was sure I hadn't
blinked. Nothing at
all had fallen into the
pool of water, and yet it *looked* and *sounded* as if something had. I stared at the pool of water, watching the
circular ripples spread outward to the edge of the basin,
distorting the reflection of the stained glass above. I
glanced quickly at Poog and saw that he was staring at
the water just as intently as Queen Pwip.

"Alia Rellapor," Queen Pwip said suddenly in a
hushed voice.

It startled me to hear that name again. My stomach
tightened and I felt the hairs stand up on the back of
my neck.

"You're trying to find Alia Rellapor's castle. You
need to rescue someone."

"Th-that's right," I answered. My heart was beating

very quickly now. It was a very weird feeling, like being excited and scared at the same time.

"Don't worry, Akiko," she said, never once taking her eyes off the pool of water. "You'll reach her castle eventually. But it won't be easy."

PLIP!

The surface of the water once again rippled gently outward from the center.

"There's a wall," Queen Pwip announced in a slightly louder voice.

"A wall?"

"You must climb the wall and cross the bridge," she continued mysteriously. She seemed to be describing things she could see in the water, things that were completely invisible to me. I looked over at Poog. Could he see things in the water too? It was hard to tell.

PLIP!

"Throck," Queen Pwip continued. "Beware of a man named Throck."

I certainly didn't like the sound of *that*. I almost wished she wouldn't tell me about the bad stuff. I tried to memorize all the things she was saying, though, so that I could tell Spuckler and Mr. Beeba all about it when we were done.

PLIP!

"There is also a friend," Queen Pwip said. "He will help you."

"Whose friend?" I asked "*My* friend?"

For the first time Queen Pwip shifted her gaze from the pool of water and looked directly into my eyes. I saw a brief look of annoyance that quickly softened into an expression of great patience.

"No questions, Akiko," she said again. "Only answers."

She returned her gaze to the water and waited.

PLIP!

"The boy," she said, the purple light reflecting up into her face. "The boy you're trying to reach. He's in good health. But he's sad and very lonely. He's almost given up hope of ever being rescued."

Several more minutes passed without a sound.

"That's all I see," Queen Pwip announced. I let out a loud sigh and leaned back against the wall behind me. Poog turned to me with a slight smile and blinked once or twice.

PLIP!

"Wait," Queen Pwip whispered urgently. "There's more."

My heart felt like it skipped a beat. I closed my eyes and hoped she wouldn't say anything scary.

"Your parents," she said. Her face was nearly expressionless, but there was a warmer tone in her voice than before. "I see your parents, Akiko."

"You *do*?" I asked excitedly. Suddenly my mind was racing. There were so many things I wanted to know!

"What are they—" I stopped myself in midsentence. "Sorry. No questions."

Queen Pwip looked at me and smiled.

"Well . . . ," she said, choosing her words carefully, "I don't see how *one* question could do anybody any harm."

I swallowed and thought hard. One question. I'd better make it a good one. I thought and thought and finally settled on the one thing I most wanted to know.

"Are they okay?"

Queen Pwip stared into the water and smiled.

"They're fine, Akiko," she answered. "They're just fine. It's very sweet of you to worry about them."

I sighed and sat back again. Queen Pwip continued staring into the pool. I really wished I could see what she saw.

"They would be very proud of you, Akiko, if they knew about all the things you've done since you came here," she said, sounding almost as if *she* was the one who was proud of me. "Not every child could do what you've done."

My face became very warm. I was blushing again. Poog and Queen Pwip were no longer looking at the pool; they were both looking at me.

"You need to keep going, though, Akiko," Queen Pwip said with a serious look. "It's natural for you to think about your parents, to wonder how they are and what they're doing. But don't forget about that little boy out there in Alia Rellapor's castle. He's depending on you to rescue him."

"I'll . . . I'll do my best, Queen Pwip," I said.

"I know you will," she replied, smiling brightly and blinking. "I know you will."

Chapter 20

One by one we crawled out of the little room. Queen Pwip led Poog and me back to the front of the palace grounds, where Admiral Frutz was waiting.

"Admiral Frutz," she said to him, "I've got a little job for you. I want you and your men to draw up a map showing the way from here to the Great Wall of Trudd. My friends need some help in getting where they're going."

Admiral Frutz winced a little when he heard Queen Pwip refer to us as friends, but he didn't hesitate to follow orders.

"I'll have my men get to work on it immediately, Your Majesty!" he said, clicking his heels and marching away from us.

"Make it a *big* map, Frutzy!" she shouted after him. "I don't want them straining their eyes!"

She turned back to me and smiled.

"Come now, it's time for that tea I promised you," she said.

"Um, Queen Pwip," I said, remembering Mr. Beeba and the others, "are you sure we couldn't invite the rest of my friends to join us? I think I'd enjoy the tea a lot more if I could share it with them."

Queen Pwip looked at me and rubbed her chin as if she was taking the matter into serious consideration. Actually, it looked as if she was *acting* like she was taking the matter into consideration. I don't think Queen Pwip was the sort of person to worry very much about breaking her own rules.

"You're quite right, Akiko," she said with a wink. "The more the merrier!"

We strolled around the palace wall until we came to the spot where Spuckler, Gax, and Mr. Beeba were working. They had already finished polishing about half the domes. Queen Pwip was very impressed.

"My, my!" she exclaimed. "I ought to put you three on the payroll!"

I smiled and tried to imagine how Admiral Frutz would have reacted to *that*.

"That's enough work," she continued. "Come join us for tea!"

"*Thank* you, Your Majesty!" Mr. Beeba cried, obviously very happy to give his arms a rest. He and the others left their cleaning rags where they were and walked with us into the palace gardens.

There in the middle of an ornate stone patio stood a miniature table covered with delicious-looking cakes and cookies. Queen Pwip asked us to sit down, apologizing for the lack of chairs.

"I've got all manner of chairs, actually," she explained, "but none in your *size*, you see."

We all sat down on the ground and watched as one of Queen Pwip's servants brought in a tray loaded with a beautiful ceramic teapot, six little cups, and six little saucers. Queen Pwip then proceeded to pour us each a

hot cup of pink tea, carrying the cups and saucers to us one at a time. It occurred to me that Gax and Poog wouldn't actually *drink* any tea, but it was very kind of her to remember them, anyway.

She then brought us each a plateful of brightly colored cakes and cookies. To the Sprublians, it must have seemed an enormous amount of food, but to us, of course, it was no more than the tiniest snack imaginable. It was quite good, though, and we all did our best to show how much we enjoyed it. As our little teatime came to a close, Queen Pwip stood up to make an announcement.

"Firstly, I'd like to thank you all for paying us a visit here in the Sprubly Islands," she said. "I do hope you'll come back again soon. Secondly, I want to wish you all the best of luck with this mission of yours. That little boy is very lucky to have such a capable rescue team coming out to save him."

I couldn't help wondering if she knew how badly off course this rescue team had actually gotten. If she had known, I'm sure *capable* wouldn't have been the word she would have chosen.

"Thank you, Queen Pwip," I said. "Without you we'd be completely lost right now. If we make it to Alia Rellapor's castle—"

"*When*, dear," she interrupted, smiling. "When."

"*When* we make it to Alia Rellapor's castle, it'll be mostly thanks to you."

Just then Admiral Frutz and a dozen or so of his men returned, carrying their neatly drawn map. It was only about six inches square, but to them it was like carrying an enormous tent. Considering how little time they'd had to draw the map, it was a very impressive piece of work.

"Thank you, Frutz," Queen Pwip said, inspecting the map carefully. "This will get them headed in the right direction."

Mr. Beeba and I leaned over to take a better look.

"I'll have Admiral Frutz lead you as far as this point," Queen Pwip said, indicating a spot on the map. "Then you'll follow this road until you reach the Great Wall of Trudd."

"The Great Wall of Trudd, eh?" Mr. Beeba asked. "Sounds rather imposing."

"Oh, it is, Mr. Beeba," she answered, nodding solemnly, "it most certainly is. The wall was built centuries ago by Big People like yourselves. Getting to the other side of it will require all the strength and wits you can muster."

"Don'tcha worry, Queen Pwip," Spuckler joined in confidently. "We got plenty of strength, and our wits ain't too bad neither."

Queen Pwip laughed loudly and warmly.

"I know better than to worry about *you*, Spuckler," she said cheerfully. "You're a one-man rescue team all by yourself.

"Still," she continued, pointing at me, "you're lucky to have Akiko along. She's a very remarkable girl."

"That she is," Mr. Beeba said proudly.

Chapter 21

I would have been perfectly happy to stay there for the rest of the day, but I could see that the others were itching to get on with the mission. I guess I was ready to move on too. The things Queen Pwip had told me had made me very curious, and now I was eager to see what would happen next. What she'd told me about my parents had also given me a new way of looking at the mission. I don't know if it makes a whole lot of sense or not, but I had this vision of my parents watching over me as we prepared to take off on the next part of our journey. I knew Queen Pwip was right. They really *would* be proud if they could see the things I was doing.

Queen Pwip led us to a gate behind the palace. She ordered Admiral Frutz and a small group of his soldiers to lead us to the edge of the city. She was getting ready to say goodbye when suddenly she seemed to change her mind.

"I'll go along with you," she said with a quaver in her voice, "just as far as old Frutzy here."

Admiral Frutz bristled a bit, perhaps at the nickname.

"Are you sure, Your Majesty?" he asked in a hushed tone. "It's highly irregular."

"Of *course* I'm sure!" she insisted. "Come on, then. Off we go!"

And so Queen Pwip joined us as we left the palace behind and marched toward the edge of the city. I felt a little lump in my throat as I realized we'd soon have to say goodbye to Queen Pwip. I knew I'd miss her. I'd probably even miss Admiral Frutz a little too.

We passed through one street and then another. People stopped and stared and pointed. At first I thought they were excited about seeing us, but then I realized it was Queen Pwip they were staring at. I guess she hardly ever left her palace except on special occasions, and so people thought it was a very big deal to see her out there marching down the street.

After a while the houses got smaller and the big street we were walking on turned into a wide dirt road. Admiral Frutz and Queen Pwip led us to the top of a slope and then stopped.

"I'm afraid this is as far as we can go," Queen Pwip said with a sigh.

"We quite understand, Your Majesty," Mr. Beeba replied with great politeness.

"Thanks for everything, Queen Pwip," I said. "I don't know how we can ever repay you for your kindness. . . ."

"Nonsense!" she replied with a smile. "I haven't had so much fun in years! Now go on and get moving. I hate long goodbyes!"

We all waved and called out as we walked down the slope that led into the countryside. Big clouds rolled by overhead, casting long shadows that crept slowly over the hills and forests on either side of us.

I kept turning around to wave goodbye. Queen Pwip

and Admiral Frutz were so tiny to begin with, it didn't take very long before we could hardly see them at all. Finally we passed over a hill that blocked our view back to the city. Just before we did, though, I waved vigorously and called out one more time.

"Goodbye, Queen Pwip! Goodbye, Admiral Frutz!" I cried. "We'll never forget you!"

To my surprise, I realized that I was almost beginning to cry. It wasn't a sad cry, though. It wasn't exactly happy, either. It was a feeling that I don't really know the name for. Just a really *emotional* feeling. As I looked around at Mr. Beeba, and Spuckler, and Poog, and Gax, I could hardly believe all the amazing things we'd been through together already. And as I looked down the long, rough road that stretched ahead of us, I found myself becoming more and more curious about the things that were yet to come.

The adventure continues in

and the Great Wall of Trudd

AND SEE WHERE IT ALL BEGAN:

Join Akiko and her crew on the Planet Smoo!

When fourth-grader Akiko comes home from school one day, she finds an envelope waiting for her. It has no stamp or return address and contains a *very* strange message. . . .

At first Akiko thinks the message is a joke, but before she knows it, she's heading a rescue mission to find the King of Smoo's kidnapped son, Prince Frop-toppit. Akiko the head of a rescue mission? She's too afraid to be on the school's safety patrol!

Read the following excerpt from *Akiko and the Planet Smoo* and see how the adventure began.

Chapter 1

My name is Akiko. This is the story of the adventure I had a few months ago when I went to the planet Smoo. I know it's kind of hard to believe, but it really did happen. I swear.

I'd better go back to the beginning: the day I got the letter.

It was a warm, sunny day. There were only about five weeks left before summer vacation, and kids at school were already itching to get out. Everybody was talking about how they'd be going to camp, or some really cool amusement park, or whatever. Me, I knew I'd be staying right here in Middleton all summer, which was just fine by me. My dad works at a company where they hardly ever get long vacations, so my mom and I have kind of gotten used to it.

Anyway, it was after school and my best friend, Melissa, and I had just walked home together as always. Most of the other kids get picked up by their parents or take the bus, but Melissa and I live close enough to walk to school every day. We both live just a few blocks away in this big apartment building that must have been built about a hundred years ago. Actually I think it used to be an office building or something, but then somebody cleaned it up and turned it into this fancy new apartment building. It's all red bricks and tall windows, with a big black fire escape in the back. My parents say they'd rather live somewhere out in the suburbs, but my dad has to be near his office downtown.

Melissa lives on the sixth floor but she usually comes up with me to the seventeenth floor after school. She's got three younger brothers and has to share her bedroom with one of them, so she doesn't get a whole lot of privacy. I'm an only child and I've got a pretty big bedroom all to myself, so that's where Melissa and I spend a lot of our time.

On that day we were in my room as usual, listening to the radio and trying our best to make some decent card houses. Melissa was telling me how cool it would be if I became the new captain of the fourth-grade safety patrol.

"Come on, Akiko, it'll be good for you," she said. "I practically promised Mrs. Miller that you'd do it."

"Melissa, why can't somebody *else* be in charge of the safety patrol?" I replied. "I'm no good at that kind of stuff. Remember what happened when Mrs. Antwerp gave me the lead role in the Christmas show?"

Melissa usually knows how to make me feel better about things, but even she had to admit last year's Christmas show was a big disaster.

"That was different, Akiko," she insisted. "Mrs. Antwerp had no idea you were going to get stage fright like that."

"It was worse than stage fright, Melissa," I said. "I can't believe I actually forgot the words to 'Jingle Bells.'"

"This isn't the Christmas show," she said. "You don't

have to memorize any words to be in charge of the safety patrol." She was carefully beginning the third floor of a very ambitious card house she'd been working on for about half an hour.

"Why can't I just be a *member* of the safety patrol?" I asked her.

"Because Mrs. Miller needs a leader," she said. "I'd do it, but I'm already in charge of the softball team."

And I knew Melissa meant it, too. She'd be in charge of *everything* at school if she could. Me, I prefer to let someone else be the boss. Sure, there are times when I wish I could be the one who makes all the decisions and tells everybody else what to do. I just don't want to be the one who gets in trouble when everything goes wrong.

"Besides," Melissa continued, "it would be a great way for you to meet Brendan Fitzpatrick. He's in charge of the boys' safety patrol." One thing about Melissa: No matter what kind of conversation you have with her, one way or another you end up talking about boys.

"What makes you so sure I *want* to meet Brendan Fitzpatrick?" The card house I'd been working on had completely collapsed, and I was trying to decide whether it was worth the trouble to start a new one.

"Trust me, Akiko," she said with a big grin, "*everyone* wants to meet Brendan Fitzpatrick."

"I don't even like him," I said, becoming even more anxious to change the subject.

"How can you not like him?" she asked, genuinely puzzled. "He's one of the top five cute guys in the fourth grade."

"I can't believe you actually have a *list* of who's cute and who isn't."

That was when my mom knocked on my door. (I always keep the door shut when Melissa's over. I never know when she's going to say something I don't want my mom to hear.)

"Akiko, you got something in the mail," she said, handing me a small silvery envelope.

She stared at me with this very curious look in her eyes. I don't get letters very often. "Are you sure you don't want this door open?" she asked. "It's kind of stuffy in here."

"Thanks, Mom. Better keep it closed."

It was all I could do to keep Melissa from snatching the letter from me once my mom was out of sight. She kept stretching out her hands all over the place like some kind of desperate basketball player, but I kept twisting away, holding the envelope against my chest with both my hands so she couldn't get at it.

"It's from a boy, isn't it? I knew it, I knew it!" she squealed, almost chasing me across the room.

"Melissa, this is *not* from a boy," I said, turning my back to get a closer look at the thing. My name was printed on the front in shiny black lettering, like it had been stamped there by a machine. The envelope was made out of a thick, glossy kind of paper I'd never seen before. There was no stamp and no return address. Whoever sent the thing must have just walked up and dropped it in our mailbox.

"Go on! Open it up!" Melissa exclaimed, losing patience.

I was just about to, when I noticed something printed on the back of the envelope:

TO BE READ BY AKIKO AND NO ONE ELSE

"Um, Melissa, I think this is kind of private," I said, bracing myself. I knew she wasn't going to take this very well.

"What?" She tried again to get the envelope out of my hands. "Akiko, I can't believe you. We're best friends!"

I thought it over for a second and realized that it wasn't worth the weeks of badgering I'd get if I didn't let her see the thing.

"All right, all right. But you have to promise not to tell anyone else. I could get in trouble for this."

I carefully tore the envelope open. Inside was a single sheet of paper with that same shiny black lettering:

DEAR AKIKO:
WE ARE COMING
TO GET YOU. MEET US
OUTSIDE YOUR BEDROOM
WINDOW TONIGHT AT
8:00. DON'T FORGET
YOUR TOOTHBRUSH.

And that's all it said. It wasn't signed, and there was nothing else written on the other side.

"Outside my window? On the seventeenth floor?"

"It's got to be a joke." Melissa had taken the paper out of my hands and was inspecting it closely. "I think it *is* from someone at school. Probably Jimmy Hampton. His parents have a printing press in their basement or something."

"Why would he go to so much trouble to play a joke on me?" I said. "He doesn't even *know* me." I had this strange feeling in my stomach. I went over to the window and made sure it was locked.

"Boys are weird," Melissa replied calmly. "They do all kinds of things to get your attention."

About the Author and Illustrator

Mark Crilley was raised in Detroit, where his parents sometimes wondered if he wasn't from another planet. After graduating from Kalamazoo College in 1988, he traveled to Taiwan and Japan, where he taught English to students of all ages for nearly five years. It was during his stay in Japan in 1992 that he created the story of Akiko and her journey to Smoo. First published as a comic book in 1995, the bimonthly Akiko series has since earned Crilley numerous award nominations, as well as a spot on *Entertainment Weekly*'s "It List" in 1998. *Akiko on the Planet Smoo*, Crilley's first work of fiction for young readers, was published by Delacorte Press.

Mark Crilley lives with his wife, Miki, and their son, Matthew, just a few miles from the streets where he was raised.